MINIONS OF THE SHADOW

MINIONS OF THE SHADOW

WILLIAM GRAY BEYER

COVER BY

LAWRENCE STERNE STEVENS

STEEGER BOOKS • 2021

CHAPTER I

RUN, CREEK, RUN

OMEGA GLARED MALEVOLENTLY. Murder, obviously, was in his eye. The left one, that is; the right one refused to cooperate. It twinkled. But it seemed that the left one was really a true barometer of his intentions, for Mark suddenly noticed that a wicked-looking, curved scimitar had appeared in Omega's hand.

Mark watched, placid and unconcerned, as a horny thumb gauged the keenness of the steel edge. Nor did he so much as smile as Omega severed the thumb neatly at the first joint.

For the interested observer—had there been one—the scene was noteworthy. Omega, aged and wrinkled, and clothed in a flowing Roman toga, beret, and spiked baseball shoes, mirrored a combination of emotions. Indignation had followed Mark's request, but that had been followed immediately with apparently uncontrollable rage—centered, of course, in the left eye. The right continued to twinkle monotonously.

Mark faced him without a qualm, his strong face expressing exactly nothing—except perhaps, strength. There was, however, a certain purposefulness about Mark's very imperturbability. He was obviously waiting for an answer, and refused to be distracted by anything.

Not even the fact that the stump of the severed thumb immediately sprouted a hollyhock in full bloom, nor the even more startling fact that the disinherited thumb did not fall to the ground but rather soared erratically off in winged flight, affected him in the least.

Mark and Omega, being very invisible, landed
right in the middle of a murder scene

It was the last, perhaps, which might have indicated to that interested observer a possibility of error in assuming that Omega's left eye was the correct one to believe. The twinkle, maybe, was the proper indication of Omega's state of mind. But almost as soon as this poor, befuddled observer had concluded that such was the case, he would have again revised his opinion. For Omega lashed out abruptly with the scimitar and snicked off the tip of Mark's nose.

At this point, perhaps, the interested observer would have gone quietly mad. For the partial proboscis also took wing and immediately engaged the thumb in mortal combat. It was a foolish thing to do, for the thumb was much larger and apparently more ferocious. It had grown a wicked pair of mandibles when nobody was looking. In no time at all it had the nose-end in a death grip, squeezing unrelentingly, in spite of the pitiful nasal whines for mercy which rent the air.

Yes, the opinion is herewith set forth that the interested observer would have lost his grip on whatever vestige of sanity remained.

The left eye continued to glare balefully as Omega growled: "I won't do it!"

Mark looked cross-eyed down the length of his nose, and was reassured to see that it was whole again. "I only asked a favor," he pointed out, in a slightly injured tone of voice. "I don't see why you have to get so upset. If you don't want to do it, say so. I won't ask you again."

"I *did* say so," snorted Omega. "I repeat: I won't do it!"

Mark didn't answer. He gazed sadly at the fallen gladiator which had been the end of his own nose. The thumb was still worrying the corpse, after the manner of a cat with a mouse. Some of the fire went out of Omega's left eye as he contemplated Mark's doleful expression. He quickly regained it, however, as Mark glanced up and shook his head sadly, the picture of disappointed disillusionment.

"Okay," he said, resignedly. "Forget it."

"It wasn't fair to ask," said Omega, now on the defensive. "You know the trouble I get in when I travel back in time. A *friend* wouldn't make such a request," he added, pointedly.

MARK SUDDENLY, snapped out of his dejected attitude. "Now who's being unfair?" he wanted to know. "I only asked you to go back six thousand years or so. Back before I went to sleep. That wouldn't get you in any trouble.

"You told me you only got in difficulties when you go far enough back to meet yourself when you still lived in your original body. Like the time when you caught yourself merging with yourself and had to live your whole life over again. So you're just splitting hairs. That was over fifty thousand years ago."

"I know, I know," said Omega, plaintively. "But I was in existence six thousand years ago, even if I didn't have a body. And I wouldn't want to have to do it all over again."

"Your original form wasn't in existence then," Mark argued. "You were nothing but a disembodied intelligence at that time."

"Of course. But I was there just the same. How do I know I won't merge anyhow." He paused, apparently thinking of a new argument. "And if you remember back, my fine fellow, it was me that wakened you after you got that dose of sleeping potion that was masquerading as an anesthetic. Suppose I should go back, as you request, and suppose I merge with myself as I was then and suppose I get mad and refuse to awaken you again? You know it's no fun having to live your life over again, and doing everything exactly the same way you did it the first time, just to make history come out right. I'm not so sure I'd do it again. I like fun!"

Mark was silent for a long minute. The thought was appalling. If Omega should accidentally merge and refuse to awaken him from his long sleep of suspended animation, nothing he had accomplished in the fifteen years since his awakening would exist. It was confusing, in a way.

He *had* been awakened, hadn't he? And he had met Nona and married her and had two kids, hadn't he? How could all that be undone? He'd almost civilized the modern Vikings, and he'd freed The Land of the Brish, and he'd come back to present benighted America and made a pretty nice place of the modern city of Detroit.

Could all that be cast into the limbo if Omega decided to live his life in a different manner? It sounded slightly screwy, on the surface. He said as much.

"Oh it does, does it?" Omega's voice dripped sarcasm. "Well I'm a screwy guy, brother. Look—I'll take you back about an hour, and then we'll see what you say."

Mark braced himself, but it was too late. He felt a sudden sinking feeling, a complete absence of light, then a sensation of rapid motion. That stopped after a moment, and abruptly his vision returned. He looked around and discovered he was about a mile from where he'd been a second before. There was a stream beside him, cutting its way through a slight rise in the plain near the city. He looked toward the direction where he knew he had stood one hour before, but found that the rise blocked his view.

It was at that moment that he discovered he didn't have a body. Nor a head, either, for that matter. He was now no more than a disembodied intelligence. He could see all right, and he could hear, the rippling of the stream was quite audible. But no body! He also realized that Omega was in a similar state, though that was quite natural for him.

There was a difference, though. Ordinarily he couldn't sense the presence of Omega unless that being let it be known he was in the vicinity. But now he could sense him. Omega was right beside him. A certain tension—probably the thought waves which composed him—indicated his presence.

"How do you like it?" The question was only a thought, but he heard it as a voice.

"Be handy when it rains," he thought back. "But what does it prove?"

"I'll show you in a minute," Omega answered. "Right now you and I are a little distance down this stream. That's why I brought you up here. So we wouldn't merge with ourselves. And right now that other 'you' is making up an alleged mind as to whether to request me to take him back in time to visit some old acquaintances. And I'm making up my mind to refuse. Right?"

"The first half's right," Mark conceded. "Which means that you were reading my mind at the time. Shame on you."

"Dull reading," said Omega, with a mental sniff. "But the point is that one hour from now, our point of departure in time, you and the body I had assumed were standing at a distance of about twenty feet from that stream. Right?"

Mark didn't see what was coming, but he answered: "Right."

"All right, then. Now I'm going to use some of nature's abundant power to alter the course of the creek. Watch."

CHAPTER II

BRACE YOURSELF
FOR THE PAST

MARK WATCHED AND marveled. He knew that Omega, by mental control, could manipulate the sub-cosmic forces which pervade all space, but he didn't often get a chance to watch him do it. He saw tons of earth melt away as Omega caused a deep ravine to be cut through the little hill which stood between their present position and the place where they had been.

He refrained from looking toward that other Mark, afraid his disembodied intelligence would be forced by some unknown law to merge with that other self.

Instead he watched the ravine extend itself toward the creek. When they met, the inevitable happened. The waters of the stream were given an easier path to follow and they followed it. They flowed through the ravine.

"Now," said Omega. "Let's merge. Head down that ravine, and you'll find yourself merging, whether you want to or not."

Mark discovered that he needed no more than a thought to move his bodiless form. With Omega at his side he sped down the new creek bed, in advance of the water. As they moved, Omega extended the ravine along with them. But Mark didn't notice. He had sighted his own body, standing in conversation with the aged one in the Roman toga.

Unaccountably he felt drawn to it, and noticed that his speed had increased, hurtling him toward it. In a space of a few seconds he had reached it, and suddenly found himself looking through its eyes. He found himself stopping in the middle of a sentence he couldn't remember beginning, and turned to Omega in astonishment.

Omega grinned. "You could probably remember what you were saying at this moment, if you thought a while. But it doesn't matter. The point is: Are you going to stay here and get wet?"

Mark, suddenly alarmed, turned to face the creek. As he guessed, it was dry; or rather, slightly muddy. Glancing quickly back, he saw that the new course of the stream would pass directly over the spot on which he was standing. And furthermore, it would arrive in a matter of seconds. Hastily he moved away to higher ground.

Not that it would have been dangerous to remain, for there was only a foot or two of water winding its way downward. But he didn't relish getting his sandals soaked. Omega moved with him, grinning gleefully.

Mark stopped, safely out of range of the new creek, and faced the aged caricature of a man. "Are you imitating a gargoyle with Cheshire cat tendencies?" he asked. "Or has something gone over my head?"

"The latter, I assure you," Omega drawled. "It happens again and again. Perhaps I should remind you that less than a half hour has passed since we went back that hour. Now it should occur to you that already that hunk of protoplasm you inhabit is doing things it didn't do originally during that hour. And do you intend to be standing in the middle of the creek, getting your tootsies wet, when the hour is up? Or did I change history by changing the course of the stream?"

Mark scratched his head. It didn't itch, but it just seemed the thing to do. There was something he should grasp...

"Ah," he chortled. "But you took me along with you back in time, and when I merged with myself I made my body do something it hadn't done originally. Suppose I hadn't gone with you? Then I would have been at the original place at the end of that hour and—"

Omega chuckled gleefully. "Sure," he said derisively. "You'd still be standing over there in the water. You wouldn't be moving out of the way when it suddenly began to creep up your ankles. You'd stand there, getting wet for the next half hour."

MARK FROWNED. There was no doubt of it. Omega had changed history. Even at this very instant he had been standing in a different place. If Omega hadn't decided to demonstrate, he would be standing there a half hour from now. He was, in fact…

It was all very confusing. Suppose Omega hadn't made that little excursion in time. This creek was pretty well stocked with trout and he often fished at the very place where there now was a shallow furrow of drying creek-bed. A week from now, maybe tomorrow, he would be fishing in it. But Omega had made his excursion, and there wouldn't be any water in that furrow.

"Then I'm to infer that all these fifteen years I've lived…" He hesitated momentarily, but went on again. "And those two kids of mine—they'd just cease to exist if you went back in time and decided not to awaken me?"

Omega chuckled again, giving Mark a disquieting feeling that he was talking to omnipotence or something very near it. "Exactly," Omega said. "You, and all the things you have done would be as if they had never existed. Maybe they don't exist anyway," he added reflectively. "Maybe you're only here because I thought of you. Anyway, I guess you don't feel like taking a chance on oblivion, just to see a few of your old friends."

Mark looked at the new creek, musingly, then suddenly smiled. "I'll take a chance," he said. "Take me to my home town, just prior to the time of that operation which ended in my protracted nap. I've got a friend there by the name of Harvey Nelson. I'd like to see him."

Omega was startled, a thing which seldom happened. He looked at Mark searchingly for a few seconds. Then he smiled.

"I see," he said. "You lived in New York, about ninety miles away, at that time. So you figure you won't meet yourself. And I was watching the results of that operation, just for something to do. I told you that once, didn't I? But how do you know that

I wasn't in your home town too, somewhere around that time? I get around, you know."

"Were you?"

It was Omega's turn to frown. "I don't believe—" he began. "Aw Mark, don't be foolish about this thing. If you go back, you'll only get more homesick. And you won't be able to make yourself heard, anyway. You haven't sufficient mental control of the forces involved. And even if you had, you'd only scare the pants off somebody. I can't give you another body, you know. Not in the past, at any rate."

"I could see and hear, couldn't I?"

"Sure," Omega said. "Just as you could a little while ago. But I advise against it. You'll wish you hadn't…"

MARK FELT the same feeling of faintness, accompanied by the blackout, which he had experienced before. This time it lasted slightly longer, but ended just as abruptly. But the return of his vision didn't disclose anything as rustically beautiful as the landscape around the former creek.

It was beautiful, of course, but in a different way. Mark had to admit that the female figure which lay on the floor before his disembodied vision—it was quite comely.

And she was dressed to display all her pulchritude. There was only one thing wrong with her. Her throat was cut! He stared, stunned. For an instant he couldn't marshal his brain—or the ethereal pattern which functioned as a brain—to bring him up to the present, or even the past. The sight of such a lovely creature, cut off in the prime… Dimly he realized that someone was speaking.

"…Thanks a lot for your help. But keep yourself available in case I need you."

He looked up and saw the speaker. He was a small, dapper man who had the air of a professional of some sort. His words, however, indicated that he must be of the police. Mark was attracted by a movement at the door, and turned in time to see the backs of a man and woman pass through it. He recognized them immediately.

"That's Harvey Nelson," he exclaimed. "The girl's the one he's being going with for several years, but hasn't gotten anywhere with."

"Terrible English," Omega remarked. "Well, take a good look at him, because we're going back where we came from. I'm nervous."

Mark started to move toward the now-closed door, knowing full well he would pass right through it, in his present bodiless state, but abruptly stopped at the sound of another voice.

"Hadn't you better put a tail on him?" it said. "It'd be a swell gag to come back and discover a body you'd killed an hour ago."

The dapper man snorted. "You state cops," he said. "He'll be looking for a tail. I know where I can get hold of him. I'll put a man on him later, when he's not looking for one."

Mark shot a mental message to Omega to wait. "Nelson's suspected of this murder," he explained. "We've got to do something. Let's hear…"

"I'll bet his story will check," remarked another man.

The dapper man sneered. "We'll see," he said, enigmatically.

Mark was alarmed. "He thinks he knows something to use against Nelson," he told Omega. "I know these cops. If they've got a good suspect, they don't bother to look further, just marshal all the evidence they can, whether it's the right man or not."

Omega groaned audibly. "So what?" he inquired wearily.

"Let's go back further in time and see what caused the present state of affairs," Mark suggested. "Maybe we can take a hand."

"We?" asked Omega sarcastically. "Why it takes half my mental strength to drag you around with me. We're not in the present, you know. We're in the past, and it requires a special effort to even stay here. Unless, of course, we should happen to meet up with ourselves. Then we'd stay whether we wanted to or not. I tell you I'm getting nervous!"

"Calm yourself," said Mark. "We're almost a hundred miles

away from our old selves. We're safe. We can't merge. Come on, be a sport. You wouldn't want to see an innocent man convicted of a crime, would you?"

"How do I know he's innocent? A friend of yours. Oh, all right. We'll go back a few more days and see what led up to this. But I don't mind telling you it's hard to keep in one spot very long, this far back in time, let alone change events to any extent.

"You must remember that after six thousand years, the fabric of time has set itself quite firmly. And to make any change which would nullify things which have existed so long requires a lot of energy. And besides, I'm a mere shadow of myself, this far back. All right, brace yourself!"

In the instant before oblivion again claimed him, Mark noticed a husky man in a blue civilian suit, leaving by the door Nelson and the woman had gone through. Then darkness descended.

CHAPTER III

WHO'S LOONEY NOW?

FOWLER'S THIRD CHIN took on a crafty look. It was, of course, only aping the rest of his face—if the thing could be called a face at all. Pembroke, the party leader, considered it more like a slightly deteriorated pumpkin, than a physiognomy.

True, the thing had a nose, and most pumpkins are totally without noses: and then too, there was the multiplicity of chins—another unpumpkinlike attribute. But, on the other hand, it did bulge on all sides, and had a slightly yellowish cast— probably something to do with the liver.

It was a versatile thing, sometimes mirroring a benign, paternal emotion; or again expressing deep-felt horror or repugnance—as when viewing with alarm—or possibly portraying cheerful martyrdom. It all depended on the subject being discussed.

Right now it was crafty, which meant that it was crafty all over, from the most elevated lock of snowy hair to the nethermost chin.

Pembroke shuddered slightly as he brushed the tips of his fingers together and regarded his highly polished nails.

"It's in the bag, boss," said Fowler's hearty voice. "Nelson will turn the trick. I've got him eating out of my hand."

He waved a hand.

"I hope you're right," said Pembroke. "You're well aware that we can't afford to lose this time. If Nelson won't play ball, we'll make him see things our way."

"No, no, no!" wailed Fowler, all three chins registering agitation. "Nelson trusts me. That's why he takes my suggestions. But for God's sake, don't try to force him!

PEMBROKE STROKED the sleeve of his coat with finger nails which were beyond improvement as far as luster was concerned. "All right," he intoned. "You'll get a chance to work out on him first. Persuasion is the better course if it'll do the trick. But I can't forget that Nelson's been acting up a bit lately. That committee meeting last week…"

"Aw boss," entreated Fowler. "He didn't do that. I was looking right at him, and his feet were tucked under the chair. He never moved them!"

Pembroke shook his head doubtfully. "The committeemen didn't think so. And neither did the mayor. As soon as I pulled that bass drum off his head he pointed a finger at Nelson and said he'd been kicked."

"He must have tripped," hazarded Fowler. "Some of that metal work around the footlights was loose. And anyway, it made a hit with the committeemen. They got a kick out of old Picklepuss poking his head in that drum."

Pembroke allowed his face to come somewhere near a smile. "So did I," he confessed. "But the fact remains that Nelson was the only one who could have done it. He was sitting right back of His Honor. Then of course there was that matter of the governor's daughter…"

"She liked it, didn't she?"

"She didn't like Nelson denying it," retorted Pembroke. "Why I even heard the smack of that kiss myself!"

"You were sitting alongside her too, weren't you?" inquired Fowler meaningly. "It must have been pretty dark in that theater."

Pembroke flushed. "You're not insinuating that I—"

"No, no, no!" Fowler denied. "Only she's a pretty neat looking frill, just the same."

"Never mind that!" snapped Pembroke. "Now get out of here

and line up Nelson. This election's got to go our way, or we'll
be on the inside, looking out. Danvers must win the primary."

Fowler suddenly whitened. He knew the chief was right.
There were certain things which hadn't been covered up too well.
If a reform administration got in power, they'd start discovering
things. There would be a howl which would bring St. Peter to
the gates with a shotgun, ready to repel invaders. Fowler left the
inner sanctum, quaking inwardly.

There was a very good reason for his concealed trepidation.
He wasn't at all certain that he could bring Harvey Nelson
around to his way of thinking. For Harvey Nelson *had* been
acting a little queerly of late. Kept looking around him as if he
heard voices, or maybe was afraid of something. Then, just when
you didn't expect it, he'd pull some practical joke.

And he was clever about it too. Nobody had actually seen him
do anything. He must have learned most of these tricks while
he was on the other side. He'd never shown any sign of being a
sleight-of-hand artist before. And he invariably denied pulling
his tricks—and did it with such a bewildered air of innocence
that everybody knew right away that it was an act.

BUT IT really wasn't the tricks that had Fowler worried.
Harvey had shown signs of questioning the wisdom of his
suggestions lately. And that was bad. If Nelson ever learned the
truth… Fowler hated to think of it. Yet he had to think of it.
His bread and butter, not to mention his freedom, was at stake.

Harvey Nelson had always been such a trusting soul. He had
looked up to Fowler as being a man of integrity and civic-mind-
edness, ever since he'd been a high-school student. It seemed
incredible that Nelson could be losing his trusting faith in his
guide and mentor.

In fact, it was this unshakable belief in Fowler's honesty, more
than anything else, which had led Pembroke to place Nelson in
his position as the leader of the most thickly-populated ward in
the city. It was certain that he would allow Fowler, Pembroke's
stooge, to guide him in his inexperience.

And he had. Harvey's popularity as a war hero and all-around athlete had enabled him to garner almost all the votes in the ward, directing them as Fowler suggested. But now…

That Art Museum thing, for instance. Nelson had asked why it had taken nineteen million dollars to complete a project which a local contractor could have put up for less than six million. That had been the present mayor's baby, and Nelson had helped elect him. Fowler had said that he was a man of integrity, and, now he was having trouble, in the light of some of the administration's acts, in making Harvey keep on believing that the mayor was a paragon of virtue.

Of course the mayor didn't matter. The party was going to kick him out anyway. But it was important that Nelson keep faith in Fowler's judgment, or they'd have plenty of trouble electing the right man in the coming election.

HARVEY NELSON was a sorely pressed man. It was getting so that every time he got near anybody, something happened. And everybody promptly blamed it on him. And those voices were bothering him, too. Voice, rather; it was always the same one. And the funny thing about it was that it always sounded like his own.

That, of course, he could keep to himself. In fact he'd better keep it to himself. People who hear voices are usually locked up in the silly-shanty. But these peculiar happenings were rapidly undermining his morale.

Fleetingly it occurred to him that perhaps everybody else was going crazy. But no, that was bad. Lunatics usually thought that, and he wasn't quite ready to admit that he might belong in that category. And besides, these things frequently happened when there were too many people around. The incident of the mayor, for instance, had happened in front of a thousand people. And even the mayor himself had thought that Nelson had kicked him!

Harvey shuddered a frame-racking shudder at the thought of it. He had quite a frame to rack, too. To think that he would be accused of kicking the mayor! He had nothing but the most profound respect for His Honor. Hadn't Jim Fowler himself vouched for the man's high ideals?

Of course there was this matter of the Art Museum; but then His Honor was nothing but the innocent dupe in that. He had certainly had no hand in awarding the crooked bids which the papers were always talking about. If, indeed, there had been any crookedness. The papers were always howling about something.

"It was crooked, all right," assured the Voice.

Nelson involuntarily spun around. He knew, even as he turned, that he would see nothing but the empty living room of his bachelor quarters. But the thing was so startling that it almost always caught him off guard. Except, of course, on those occasions when the voice seemed to come from a point in front of him, and he could see instantly that no one was there.

That was one of the peculiar things about the voice. It came, on different occasions, from all thirty-two points of the compass. It seldom repeated itself twice in succession from the same direction.

The desk lamp made Harvey's shadow huge and grotesque as he hunched over the papers on the desk. He read them over carefully before signing. Fowler had once said to do that, always. But then Fowler had said that he had checked over these particular papers, and that they were okay. He'd sign them, therefore, even though some of the items listed seemed to be a bit high.

His office as county commissioner required that he affix his signature to the new budget estimates, though he really didn't know what half the items were for. But Fowler did, and that made it all right. He ought to know; most of the county money went through his hands before it was finally paid out.

Harvey thanked his stars that he had such an honest man as Jim Fowler to help him with these complicated matters.

"He's as crooked as a ram's horn!" said the voice, disgustedly.

Nelson sat up rigidly. This was too much!

"He's not!" Harvey exploded.

Then he stopped, ashamed of his lack of control. He'd let his imagination get the better of him that time. He'd actually answered the phantom voice. The voice seemed to be as surprised as he at this slip.

"Well, well, well," it said. "So you finally admit that I exist. It's about time!"

Harvey shuddered again, but not for the same reason as before. He suddenly realized that he wasn't imagining this voice. It was real! He knew it because he was thinking rapidly while the voice was talking. Before, his mind had been comparatively at rest, and the voice had crept in between his thoughts. But now—

He couldn't think of two things at the same time!

CHAPTER IV

ME AND MY SHADOW

HARVEY WAS A very level-headed man, not given to fancies at all. And when he faced a situation, he faced it, no matter how incredible it appeared on the surface. He'd run across some pretty queer things in France, and had learned to take new ones at their face value.

That, though he didn't know it, was one of the reasons why he was such a trusting soul. He didn't look for concealed motives, convinced as he was that everyone was as straightforward and honest as himself.

"Who are you?" he asked, shakily.

The voice didn't answer immediately. It seemed to be thinking over the desirability of revealing its identity.

"I'm your shadow," it finally said, a bit sullenly.

"My what?"

Harvey wheeled and looked at the wall. His shadow was there, all right, and the voice had come from behind him this time. Vainly he tried to remember where his shadow had been on some of the other occasions. But his mind was so chaotic at the moment that he couldn't be sure. Ordinarily he would have accepted the voice's words at their face value, but in the case of this entity which seemed to be given to making such obviously lying statements, he was a little wary.

"I don't lie!" said the voice, angrily. "I've tried, all right. I'd like to lie because it's one of the things you never do. But it seems that's one trait I've inherited from you. I'm glad there aren't any others."

Harvey thought that over carefully before answering. Whatever the voice was, it seemed that it could read his mind, and he didn't like that a bit. And it might be lying, in spite of the denial. He'd never heard of a shadow that talked. But then the old lady had never heard of a giraffe, either. And if the voice really was incapable of falsehood, then it meant that the mayor…

"It sounds a bit fantastic," he ventured. "Shadows are usually seen and not heard."

"I know, I know," said the voice. "I'm a bit puzzled about it myself. It's very seldom us shadows ever get strength enough to do anything. But I imagine it had something to do with that light outside the taproom, last week."

"What taproom?"

"The one on Fifty-Second Street, where you were hoisting them. There was a red neon sign with a blue ring around it. Then there was the full moon overhead. I think it was the combination of the three that brought me to life. Didn't you feel me heave up beneath your feet when I felt the strength flowing through me?"

Harvey scratched his chin reflectively. He did remember the pavement had seemed a bit unsteady that night, but had attributed it to the poor quality of the soda which had been mixed with his Scotch.

"How is it that Fowler's shadow didn't do likewise?" he wanted to know. "He was just behind me, and the same light must have struck him."

"Not quite," said the voice. "The moon moves along, you know. The combination must have been slightly different when he passed beneath the sign. Naturally a very delicate balance of light properties must be required to bring a shadow to life, or the thing would happen more often."

Harvey nodded. It all sounded very reasonable, he decided. But he didn't believe it, just the same. He was willing to accept a disembodied voice as belonging to one of the dear departed, but the idea of a shadow owning one was a little too much for him. Cautiously he turned in his chair, until he was facing the desk once more.

"I hope you don't mind my turning my back," he said. "One can't always have one's shadow in front of one, you know."

As he talked, he suddenly snapped off the desk lamp. A thin streak from a street light came from the edge of one of the curtains, but the room was otherwise in total darkness. If the voice was really his shadow, it would now be unable to answer, for there wasn't enough light to form a shadow.

"One is often skelly in one's reasoning," said the voice, from the other side of the room. "One casts a shadow, regardless of the dimness of the light which is shining on one."

Harvey swore and turned on the desk lamp. Then the thing was telling the truth. The thought suddenly appalled him. The voice had said that Fowler was a thief!

"**AND I** can prove it, too!" said the voice, exultantly. "The proof's right on your desk. Fowler figures on about ten percent of that appropriation to wind up in his bank account. The party fund will get ten more. And the taxpayers might get about fifty cents worth of value on the dollar—if they're lucky. Why don't you cut yourself in on some of that?"

Harvey listened in amazement. What a thought! If that voice really came from his shadow, the shadow certainly had none of his honesty and sense of fairness. But just the same, it might be telling the truth. Harvey Nelson turned to the papers on the desk, suddenly suspicious.

"What's crooked?" he muttered, lifting, the first sheet of the budget estimate.

"Payroll!" said the shadow derisively. "One million, four hundred thousand dollars!"

"What's the matter with that?"

"Nothing. Only that over a quarter of it is allotted to dummies. Men who don't exist. Why there's supposed to be thirty-five inspectors in the Bureau of Weights and Measures alone. How many did you ever see?"

"Well," hedged Harvey. "They're always out inspecting scales and such things. That's why I never saw them all at once."

"Phooey! You can check them, can't you? Go over to that file, and look over the list of names. There's one called Plotsky. Look at the address, and then check it with the city directory."

Harvey did as he was told, slightly mystified but willing to be shown. Plotsky, it seemed, lived in a house in the forty-one-hundred block on Second Street. The directory claimed that the block was devoted to the site of a cemetery.

"See that?" exulted the voice. "Fowler's so brazen he don't even bother to pick a real address. There's a lot of stuff like that. There's also plenty of corpses in that block who vote, too. All good party people. Why, with the in you've got..."

But Harvey was no longer listening. He dug into the budget estimate and started taking it apart, piece by piece. The voice kept quiet while he worked, and in an hour he had sliced half a million dollars from the total.

He made a separate list of the things he had cut. He wasn't sure of all of them, but some he had managed to check with the aid of his files. Tomorrow he would investigate the remainder, at his office. Then he would present the new estimate to the city council—the lowest figure since the turn of the century.

"What's the idea?" Mark inquired, with some asperity. "Do you have to plague the guy? All we want to do is to prevent him from discovering that body, so he won't be suspected. Even better—maybe you can prevent the murder altogether."

"You keep your disembodied nose out of this!" Omega retorted. "I'll do it my own way. And have a little fun in the bargain."

"But why all this stuff about being his shadow?" Mark wanted to know. "Can't you just—"

Omega chuckled eerily. "I've got to interfere a little bit at a time. So I invented the shadow idea to make it seem plausible to Nelson. There's got to be a sensible reason for not letting him act entirely of his own accord."

Mark snorted. "Sensible! A shadow coming to life!"

"I keep telling you that I don't have much power, this far back in time. Not near enough to take a significant incident and change it bodily into something else. I'm comparatively weak, so I've got to make little changes which will accumulate into a major variation from the events which really happened."

"Okay," said Mark, grudgingly. "But I don't like the idea of scaring people into thinking they've gone whacky."

CHAPTER V

LET'S GO TO TOWN

UNFORTUNATELY FOR MR. FOWLER, he chose this particularly inopportune moment to visit Harvey Nelson. He was perspiring freely from the one-flight climb and wore a jovial smile as Harvey opened the door. It changed to a look of ludicrous surprise as a big hand grasped his lapels and jerked him inside.

"Explain this!" demanded Harvey, shaking the sheaf of papers in his face. "Explain these items I've marked off!"

Fowler sputtered incoherently as he examined the papers. His face took on a look of incredulity as he perused item after item.

"My gosh, boy," he finally breathed. "We've been duped!

Harvey suddenly lost his fury. "Duped?" he asked. "How?"

But Fowler didn't answer immediately. A very realistic storm cloud was gathering on his chubby face as he strode back and forth, stopping occasionally to glare at the offending papers.

"We've been duped, son," he said, finally. "And I think I know who is behind this dastardly thing." He paused and picked up the papers, stuffing them in an inside pocket. "You leave this to me, boy. I'll move heaven and earth to uncover the guilty person!"

Harvey Nelson suddenly felt as if a great burden had been lifted from his soul. The shadow, if not actually lying, had at least been mistaken. He ignored the small voice in his ear which said: "You're being duped, you dupe!" and showed the wrathful Mr. Fowler to the door. Nobody could have been more surprised

than he when Fowler tripped on the top step and went bounc-
ing down the stairs.

Mr. Fowler sputtered to a stop at the bottom landing. He
looked up at the solicitous face of Harvey, an expression of hurt
reproach on his own face.

"You tripped me, son," he accused. "After all I've done for
you."

Harvey made hasty and horrified denials as Fowler went
down the remaining three steps to the street, shaking his head
unbelievingly. His jowls wagged to and fro, making him resem-
ble a pug dog shaking himself after an unwanted bath.

Harvey mounted the steps and entered his apartment, wrath
bubbling within him. He sat in the chair by the desk and faced
his shadow, which seemed to be leering at him flatly, from the
wall.

"You meddler!" he said in a quiet, deadly voice. "Fowler's an
honest man. Now I've hurt his feelings, thanks to YOU."

The shadow chuckled gleefully. "That ain't all that hurts," it
said. "But as for Fowler's honesty, phooey! He's a crook, just as
I said before. I can't lie, you know."

"You can be mistaken," retorted Harvey, clenching his fist and
wishing he could sock a shadow.

"I can, but I'm not," stated the shadow. "I can feel his thoughts
as well as yours, and I know he's a crook."

Harvey came alert. "You can feel his thoughts? That's absurd!"

"No it's not. When I fall on him, his thoughts get all jumbled
in with yours. I've noticed that about people ever since I came
to life."

Harvey looked mystified. "What do you mean when you fall
on him?"

"Just what I said," retorted the shadow. "When he walked
back and forth across the room, after, you showed him those
papers, he kept passing you. The light being back of you, I fell
on him. And when I did, I could read his thoughts. Kinda mixed
up, though."

Harvey stroked his chin thoughtfully. "What did he think?"

"He was scared, mostly. He kept thinking of what Pembroke would say. He was also trying to figure if it would be better to scrap the estimate and lose his graft, or to try to get rid of you, somehow, and put it through anyway. The last time I fell on him he'd made up his mind to burn all records of past years in your department, to prevent you from checking up. Then he figures to bring a bunch of men, at five dollars a throw, and introduce them to you as members of the various county bureaus under your control. He intends to account for all the dummies on the payroll."

HARVEY SLUMPED back in his chair. All the wind had been knocked out of his sails. Values he had cherished all his life were being knocked into a cocked hat. If Fowler, his idol of virtuous selflessness, was made of clay, then what things could he accept as true?

Did nothing exist as it appeared on the surface? Did he have to suspect every hearty handshake, and assume that it masked a desire to knife him in the back? Did every honest face conceal evil and wickedness?

"Of course not," the shadow told him. "Lots of people are honest, the suckers. All you have to do is forget that a face reveals anything. That don't mean that you have to go around suspecting every thing you see. It don't mean that you have to figure that everybody who acts like your friend is really your enemy. People really like you, for some reason I can't figure.

"All it means is that you shouldn't allow yourself to be impressed either way by appearances or actions. Don't be so damned guileless, just remember that everybody is looking out for himself, then you can place a better value on people's motives.

"Come on, now; snap out of it, and let's go out and have some fun. I feel like kicking a few people in the pants, or their corresponding garments."

Harvey sat quietly, not answering, his eyes focused dazedly on the wall. He noticed abstractedly that his shadow was moving, apparently dancing up and down impatiently, while he himself was motionless. But his mind was too occupied on other matters to pay any particular attention to such antics.

"He's going to burn the records," he finally said, aloud. "I'll put a stop to that!"

He sprang to his feet, and failed to notice that his shadow failed to do likewise. Perversely it crouched. Suddenly Harvey felt himself slammed back into the chair. It seemed that a pile-driver had struck him somewhere south of the short ribs.

"Listen to me, Rover Boy," hissed his shadow. "You're not going to start any campaign of reform around here. If you tried, first thing you know Pembroke would have one of his thugs slide a shiv between your ribs. And then where would I be? Nothing doing, son. I want to have some fun out of your life. Get on your coat now, and we'll go out."

> *"You're making things worse!" wailed Mark. "Now that he suspects what's going on, he'll stick his neck out and Pembroke will take a slice at it."*
>
> *"I'm stopping him from doing anything foolish, ain't I?"*
>
> *Mark groaned. He knew what Omega considered fun. He'd seen several samples of it in the past hour or so, during which he and Omega had visited Nelson several times. These visits covered more than two weeks of Nelson's life, and already Mark could see the effect they were having on his old friend.*
>
> *"But you're changing his very character," he protested. "That's not necessary."*
>
> *"Sure it is," said Omega, calmly. "He's been asleep all his life. His character needs changing."*
>
> *"I almost wish I hadn't started this thing," Mark moaned.*
>
> *"All right," said Omega brightly. "We'll quit and go back to our own time. The air's better anyway."*
>
> *"As if you cared about the air," said Mark, sulkily. "No! How about the murder? We can't leave things that way."*
>
> *"All right, then. Stop trying to interfere. And—Oh oh! Watch this!"*

CHAPTER VI

HERE GOES HARVEY!

HARVEY GOT GROGGILY to his feet. His breath was coming in short gasps, occasioned by a partial paralysis in the region of the solar plexus. And his brain was not functioning any too well. It had come as a shock that his shadow could exert such force, and especially that it could be directed against himself.

"I'm tough stuff," gloated the voice. "And listen: when we get outside, don't talk to me out loud. If you want to say anything to me, just think it. Call me Omega when you want to think anything at me. Then I'm sure to pay attention."

Out on the street Harvey found himself directed around to the garage, where he kept his car.

"We're calling on your girl friend," Omega announced. "Nice girl, by the way. Though for the life of me I can't understand what she sees in you."

Harvey steered the car out of the garage, then suddenly shot down the street in second gear, rapidly accelerating. He was doing forty before he shifted into high. This wasn't Harvey's way of driving at all. He had always been a cautious driver.

But Harvey Nelson was a hard man to lick. And Omega couldn't drive a car and concentrate on Harvey's thoughts at the same time. It was possible, therefore, for Harvey to snatch a hand from the gear-shift lever and turn off the ignition.

Then he placed the hand on the steering wheel and strove mightily to bring the car to a safe stop. He succeeded, too, and learned a new fact about his shadow's powers. Omega could

Boss Pembroke turned livid and began to pace
the floor, with Omega keeping step at his side.
Fowler was scared, but Nelson sat tight

overpower him only so long as he operated unexpectedly. When
it came to a slow tug-of-war test of strength, Harvey was the
stronger. Omega maintained a sullen silence as Harvey started
the car again and drove on at his usual discreet pace.

The sedan pulled up in front of an imposing apartment house
and parked. Nelson suddenly began to have misgivings. This
Omega person was obviously given to pranks of a most practical
nature. And Harvey was always very decorous in the presence
of the opposite sex. Especially Millicent.

"Don't worry," came the voice in his ear. "I won't do anything
she won't like."

Omega accompanied this assertion with a suggestive wallop
in the small of the back; and Nelson's wind went out with a blast
which almost bulged the windshield. He panted a little and
felt gingerly at the bruised portion of his ribs. But in spite of
a throbbing in that region he felt reassured. Omega never told

a lie, and it was altogether possible that he possessed enough personal honor to keep his promise. Harvey climbed from the car and entered the apartment house.

Omega had said that he wouldn't do anything Millicent wouldn't like. Now if he only stuck to that... Harvey entered the elevator cage before he thought of something which caused his misgivings to return.

"Omega!" he thought, as the cage began to rise. "Just what sort of thing do you suppose she likes?"

"Quiet," hissed Omega. "I know my women."

"How?"

"Easy. In the past week you've been around plenty of women. Whenever the light cast me on them, I could read their thoughts. You know—though I find no good reason for it—they all seem to admire you. Your tall, stalwart figure; that shock of sandy hair; those rugged, honest features, and especially those baby blue eyes. Son, if you weren't such a dope you could be cutting yourself in for plenty..."

TWENTY-TWENTY WAS the number on Millicent's door. Harvey rapped apologetically with his knuckles. At least he started to, but when the knuckles struck, they hit with resounding force.

"Don't be so damned timid," rasped Omega. "Women like their men to be masterful. Go in there like you knew you were welcome. Don't vacillate. Tell her you're going to take her out and hit the hot spots. I want fun!"

The voice chortled.

After a moment the door opened. Millicent, apparently on the point of retiring, was clad sketchily in a negligee which evidently hadn't been designed for warmth. Her face revealed her pleased surprise at the sight of Harvey, while the negligee revealed contours which shouldn't have been concealed anyway.

Harvey, about to open his mouth and apologize, for his unexpected call, suddenly felt himself catapulted across the threshold.

His arms, extended to catch himself, encircled her slim figure. She looked up into his eyes and tilted her face at the proper angle. Harvey kissed her. Long and lingeringly. The sensation wasn't at all disagreeable. But after a few seconds he evidently realized that this was anything but decorous behavior, and abruptly terminated the osculation. He stood, tongue-tied, while Millicent heaved a deep sigh.

"Why Harvey!" she finally exclaimed, after finding enough breath to do so.

> *"All you need now is bow, arrows, and diaper."*
>
> *"Aw, the guy needed a push. He wasn't having any fun. Too busy thinking about the proprieties and such. Before I'm through, he'll know the facts of life."*
>
> *"Could be… But two will get you five that Harvey Nelson teaches you something about sales resistance."*

Harvey turned a deep crimson. He fortunately caught himself on the point of lamely explaining that he'd tripped. That would never do now.

Millicent disengaged herself after a minute and sat weakly down on a divan. She stared quizzically at Harvey, who appeared about to sit beside her. But Mr. Nelson remembered something at that moment. Omega wouldn't make a good third on a divan. Harvey didn't trust him.

"Milly," he said, hesitantly. "Let's go out… Celebrate—or something."

Milly didn't need any coaxing. She left the room with the promise that it would take only a minute to put on her glamour.

Omega decided to intervene. "I've changed my mind," he said. "We'll stay."

"No we won't," Harvey muttered. "I've decided to go out now."

After a moment of silence Omega said: "All right. The night's young. We go out, but don't get any funny ideas about who's boss." A light dig in the ribs, accompanied by a wrenching twist of the nose, emphasized the words.

Harvey was about to try a little experiment with the lights when Millicent appeared, radiantly beautiful, and apparently as happy as she could be. She smiled at him as if they shared a delightful secret. He couldn't imagine what it was, but being a bit delirious himself, helped her on with her coat, and kissed her again before opening the door.

The sedan was about to pull away from the curb when abruptly the night was shattered by the raucous wail of a fire siren. It was followed roaringly by two red trucks, one containing sundry ladders, hooks and half-dressed men, and the other heavy with pumping equipment and bosses.

Harvey followed just as speedily with the sedan, Millicent raised a hand to stifle a scream as he cut around a corner in their wake, narrowly missing several cars.

And Harvey himself was doing the driving this time. Omega had nothing to do with it. He merely chuckled eerily in Harvey's ear, and murmured: "Doubt my word, would you? There goes the evidence—up in smoke!"

CHAPTER VII

BOSS OF THE DOUBLE CROSS

AS HARVEY HAD feared, the fire engines stopped at one of the corner entrances to the City Hall. Men armed with portable fire-extinguishers and axes boiled through the entrance. With a scream of tires he brought the sedan to a stop beside them.

Harvey Nelson was suddenly undecided as to the next move. He knew who was behind that fire, though it wouldn't do any good to say so. He'd have to prove it, and he wasn't so sure that he wanted to. Warily, he headed the sedan away from the fire-fighting equipment. He was still in a fog of mental indecision as he absently, noticed a sign, "Club Patelli," and pulled in to the curb.

Two tipsy revelers, who had been about to leave the place, stopped abruptly. Harvey's topper had raised straight in the air and then sailed toward the hat check girl's window. The tipsy two applauded noisily. Neither noticed the expression of bewilderment on Harvey's face when the hat lifted from his head.

"Thassa dandy trick," complimented one of the revelers. "Show me how you do it?"

The hat obediently sailed out of the hat check girl's hand—which happened to be directly in Harvey's shadow—and returned to his head.

"You just raise your left eyebrow," Harvey explained. "Like this!"

The hat repeated its performance, going slowly and unerringly to the girl's hands.

"S'wonderful," said the stew, blinking furiously. "Gimme my hat, gorgeous."

Harvey and Millicent followed the headwaiter to a choice table by the dance floor. A bill of fairish denomination accounted for this. Harvey had decided to make the best of things, even if he went broke in the process.

Millicent leaned confidentially over a small table, after a waiter had disappeared with their order. "How'd you do it, Harvey?" she coaxed.

"That hat trick?" Nelson breathed deeply, inhaling a heady fragrance which must have been caused by perfume doused in her hair.

"I didn't do it," he said, weakly. "I'm haunted."

"Sissy!" Omega remarked, quietly.

"Nonsense," she said, amiably.

Harvey, already in a mental turmoil, was spared the necessity of elaborating. For at that moment Fowler appeared, waddling precariously between the close-set tables. There was an urgent light in his eyes as he spotted Nelson.

"Boy!" he puffed. "Am I glad to see you! Been calling all over town, Something terrible's happened! Everything in the office is burned up. We'll have to round everybody up and get to work on a new budget estimate. There's no use trying to dig into the old one and see who's been pulling the wool over our eyes. All the records are destroyed."

Harvey looked at him sadly as he puffed to a stop. Somehow he didn't have the heart to be mad at the man. Fowler had helped him over many a tough spot; and now, in spite of his proven perfidy, Harvey found himself trying to excuse the attempt at self-preservation.

He smiled disarmingly. "That's a tough break," he said. "You'll have to get to work on another. Make sure this is a straight one. I'll help you with it myself. We won't have any dummies this time."

Fowler straightened. His face adequately revealed his injured feeling. "Why boy," he said. "You don't think that an estimate of mine would be other than—"

Harvey waved a hand. "Of course not," he interrupted. "But I'll feel better if I check everything. See you at the office."

Fowler nodded unhappily and turned to leave. At that moment he felt the sudden contact of a shoe, speeding his departure in a very undignified manner. But he didn't look back, remembering the peculiarities he had already observed in his protégée.

FOWLER DIDN'T let any grass grow under his feet. He left the night club and took a taxi directly to the home of one Felix Pembroke, the real brains of the Party. Pembroke got out of bed to receive him. Fowler babbled forth the events of the evening.

"You incompetent fool," said Pembroke finally. "He must suspect you had that fire set. You're the dumbest man I ever saw when it comes to covering your tracks."

"Some of your own tracks aren't covered so well," Fowler reminded him. "And that'll put us in a nice spot if we don't get our man in at the primaries."

Pembroke nodded grimly. "And I suppose Nelson will do the opposite of anything you suggest, from now on?"

"That's what I'm afraid of," said Fowler. "At the very least he'll check up on me. I was going to suggest that we put up a candidate who'll stand some investigating. Then we'll be fairly safe. Nelson won't turn from the Party. But he might support the reform candidate at the primaries. And if we have a man who can stand an investigation, we can trump up some stuff on the reform man, and he'll pick our man to support. How about it?"

Pembroke laughed mirthlessly. "Who?" he asked, sarcastically.

Fowler was stumped. He thought the matter over for several minutes. But every time he seemed on the verge of deciding on some prominent leader, he either remembered some shady episode which might be uncovered, or he realized that the man wouldn't appeal to the public. Either drawback might well be fatal.

Pembroke finally broke the silence. "Your plan's no good," he said. "We'll have to stick to Danvers. He can beat the reform man with the help of Nelson's ward. Mr. Nelson will have to toe the line, or else!

"In fact maybe it would better if Mr. Nelson became temporarily indisposed. You might be able to swing his ward, if you work hard enough… Sure! That's the solution! You've always relayed his orders anyway. We can do without his speeches, as long as the committeemen think he's still directing things up at the fifty-second ward. I'll get in touch with Bonzetti right away!"

Fowler paled. "No, no," he exclaimed. "Not Bonzetti! After all, the lad's been like a son to me. Give me a chance to win him over."

Pembroke shook his head. "Fool!" he said. "My way is the best. Not only will it insure the election but you can put through your original estimate for your department. Any other way you lose your gravy."

It was to Fowler's credit that he didn't hesitate. "That don't mean anything," he said. "I got plenty. Try my way first. I'll win him over. Give me a chance."

Pembroke appeared to think the request over very carefully. "All right," he finally agreed. "I'll give you a week. But remember this: If you fail, Bonzetti pulls his snatch, and you take over. And don't think you can buck me, either. A twenty-year stretch wouldn't do you much good."

Fowler left the house with his brain ticking over at a furious rate. He didn't like the crafty look he'd seen in Pembroke's eyes. It would be just like him to string him along and then send Bonzetti out to snatch Nelson anyway. The boss had a reputation for refusing to play fair with anyone—unless playing fair happened to be to his advantage.

Fowler got in the taxi, but sat still for a minute before naming a destination.

Suddenly he jumped out and mounted the terrace at the side of Pembroke's house. He padded softly to the French windows

of the room he had just quitted. Then he scurried back to the
taxi and ordered speed, back to the club where he'd come from.
The cab started out with a jolt which set his jowls to quivering
madly. Pembroke had been earnestly talking to someone over
the phone when he had looked in the windows. That could mean
only one thing. The boss was living up to his reputation. He had
only pretended to give Fowler a chance to win Nelson over, so
that he wouldn't go immediately to warn him.

And unless Fowler moved quickly, Bonzetti would descend
upon Harvey Nelson like a particularly malevolent ton of bricks.

CHAPTER VIII

HARVEY'S NECK IS OUT

HARVEY NELSON HAD another visitor at his table, almost as soon as Fowler left. A stocky man, homely, and friendly as a puppy.

"I'm Joe Patelli," he announced, grinned broadly. "I run this place. Mind if I pull up a chair for a second, Mr. Nelson?"

Harvey felt a vague sense of familiarity as he looked at the newcomer, but it didn't quite congeal into actual recognition. Joe Patelli, therefore, must be a constituent and worthy of his attention for that reason alone. Harvey felt a sense of duty toward constituents: one of the many things which set him apart as a politician. He nodded and smiled.

"This is Miss Forbes, my fiancée," he said.

Millicent raised a quizzical eye-brow, but said nothing. She was slightly stunned at the abruptness of it, and could only muster a smile as Patelli made a gallant remark about Harvey's taste.

"I'm in your ward, Mr. Nelson," he added, abruptly. "Do you mind telling me who we're going to put in, this election?"

Harvey's eyes narrowed momentarily. "It's a little early yet," he said. "Why?"

"Well," Patelli said slowly. "I got a chance to open a place in the suburbs. If I thought the reform crowd was goin' to get a hold in town, I'd do it. With the city closed tighter than a drum, a place just out of town would be a gold mine. On the other hand, it would be a waste of money if Danvers got the election. I can't run two places."

Harvey nodded. "You figure the reform crowd would be bad business, eh?"

"No doubt of it. They'd have the blue laws working in no time. You know that. Pembroke couldn't tell them what to do. It would be better if the opposition got in, meaning no offense. They'll at least play ball. But the reform crowd has got us all worried. They've almost got the Party split now. I figure it's all up to you."

"But the reform crowd wants to put a stop to vice and gambling," Millicent pointed out. "That's why they're getting so much support. People are getting tired of present conditions, according to the newspapers."

"According to the newspapers," jeered Patelli. "Lady, I'm in a position to know what I'm talking about, and that paper talk is a lot of malarkey. Right now the papers are short of news and they're making a whole lot of fuss about practically nothing, just to have something to print. As soon as somebody commits a nice, juicy murder, you won't read anything about gambling and vice."

Harvey said, "What do you mean by that?"

"Well, you know as well as me, Mr. Harvey, that there ain't any big-time gambling in town," Patelli said. "Pembroke's too greedy. As soon as an outfit begins to show a profit, he holds out his hand. They kick in for a while and then he raises the ante. First thing you know he takes all the profit out of it. And if they don't kick in, he closes them up.

"I ought to know. He drove me out of business when I had my joint. Glad he did, though. I'm making just as much here, and perfectly legitimate.

"This reform stuff is a lot of malarkey. Will it do any good to close me up? They can do it by shortening my business hours. That'll take away the profit. So what do I do? I open up again, just outside the city, and get the same trade anyway.

"Only I pay taxes to some thieving little borough on the edge of the town. That's going to help the city a lot, ain't it? Taxes will have to go up in other directions and more business leaves the town. It'll make a morgue out of this burg.

"It's nothin' to me, understand. I make money either way. I'd just like to know, so I could buy that place or turn it down."

HARVEY STARED at Patelli for a long minute before he spoke. He was once more going through a phase of mental renovation. Fowler had always spoken in the highest terms of Mr. Pembroke: pictured him as being a man of the same lofty idealism as himself. According to Fowler he had been elected to leadership in the Party because of his unselfish devotion to the cause of bettering city government.

Harvey had never liked the man personally, but had blamed himself for the dislike. He had Fowler's word that he was of the finest character. And that had been enough. It was likely that if he didn't already know of the perfidy of Fowler, he would have called Patelli a liar on the spot.

But with the disturbing knowledge that nothing Fowler had ever told him was to be relied upon... And added to that was the fact that Patelli was obviously concerned only with his own welfare, and making no attempt to influence him.

"I think you'd better stay here," said Harvey, thoughtfully.

"You're going to throw the nomination to Danvers?"

"Don't quote me," said Harvey. "I merely said you'll do better staying here. I guarantee that."

Patelli leaned back in his chair, a puzzled look on his face.

"I don't know what you mean," he finally said. "But whatever it is, it's okay with me. I'll turn down that offer. Thanks, Mr. Nelson." Patelli left the table, his face wreathed in smiles.

"You're a regular politician," Millicent remarked. "You didn't tell him anything, and he's happy. What are you going to do?"

"I don't know," said Harvey miserably. "Let's get out of here. I've got to figure some things out. We'll take a ride in the park. All right?"

"Of course," agreed Millicent. "I'll help you figure. I'm your fiancée, you know. Though I think it's a heck of a way to propose. You didn't give me a chance to turn you down!"

Harvey's knees suddenly began to quake. "I thought—" he stammered. "After all—"

"Yes, I know," said Millicent, quietly. "You kissed me, and I didn't sock you. So that proves something, doesn't it?"

"Doesn't it?" he asked, vaguely.

"Yes, dear," she replied. "It does."

OMEGA SHOWED no inclination to take charge as Harvey pulled away from the curb and headed toward the park. By the time they reached the river drive Harvey concluded that he must have fallen asleep, if shadows ever do sleep, and forgot about him.

"We made up our minds all of a sudden," he ventured as Millicent showed no inclination to open a conversation.

"Uh huh," Millicent agreed, patting him on the knee. "Except that I made mine up about three years before you did."

"Huh? Oh, no you didn't," he contradicted. "I made up my mind the instant I first saw you. It just took three years for me to tell you about it."

"Darling!" cried Millicent, almost wrecking the car as she flung her arms around his neck. Then she suddenly sobered. "But that's not what you want to talk about. Danvers is a crook, isn't he?"

Harvey covered half a mile before answering. Then: "I'm afraid he is," he replied. "Otherwise Pembroke wouldn't want him. At the very least, he's a man who will take the boss' orders. Which means graft in all the city departments, as well as the county ones."

"HARVEY! DON'T tell me there's graft in your department!"

"It's lousy with it," affirmed Harvey.

Millicent clapped her hands. "Then we'll have a honeymoon in Bermuda," she said.

Harvey's mouth popped open. "What? Wait a minute! I had nothing to do with the graft. Fowler collected it for himself and the Party. All I ever got was my salary. And that's all I want!"

"Oh," said Millicent, in a small voice.

"He's a chump!" said Omega, suddenly waking up, and speaking from the region of the windshield.

"What?" asked Millicent, absently adjusting herself to the idea of a graftless politician.

"He's a chump!" Omega repeated.

"He is not!" said Millicent, instantly jumping to the defense. "I think graft is horrible. Who said that, Harvey?"

"My shadow," Harvey explained. "I told you I was haunted. He's been with me for hours."

"I've been with you all your life," Omega remarked severely, "And a very dull existence it's been." Millicent gave a short gasp and held a hand over her mouth to stifle a scream. Shadow apparently didn't notice her fright, for he continued without a break. "Milly, you'll find it hard to believe, but this guy don't even know what the inside of a boudoir looks like! Not only that but…"

He rambled on for several minutes in the same vein, while Harvey scowled and kept his eyes glued to the road, and Millicent gradually got used to a voice speaking from thin air and settled down to listen interestedly.

"…And right now he's harboring some silly notion of making a deal with the reform gang, in which they're to promise to confine their activities to actual law breakers, such as gamblers and vice dealers, and to leave harmless night clubs and Sunday sports alone. He thinks that the noble reformers will keep promises. What a man!"

"I THINK he's nice," retorted Millicent. "He's good inside, and that's why he thinks everybody else is good. A person who suspects everybody else can't be very virtuous himself, or he wouldn't get such ideas. So there!"

"Virtue, phooey!" Omega exploded. "Who wants to be virtuous? What's it get you? Virtue is its own reward! It's got to be, says I. You can't have a good time on it. It cramps your style. Look at Horatio, here. He could be mayor by now, if he wasn't so damn virtuous. He's popular enough, but Pembroke knows he wouldn't stand for anything shady. So what is he? I ask you. What is he?"

Millicent looked at Harvey appraisingly. "What are you, darling?" she inquired.

"I'm a guy who's going to find some way of stepping on his shadow," Harvey growled. "He's getting to be a nuisance."

"Oh yeah?" exclaimed Omega with singular lack of originality.

Millicent, suddenly thinking of something, gave a short gasp. "I think he'll be worse than a nuisance," she told Harvey. "Especially after we're married."

Omega chuckled malevolently. "I'm staying," he said flatly. "I'm having lots of fun."

"*You* are," said Millicent. "But I'm not. Harvey! I just thought of something… Why not try to put Pembroke out of business? Find some evidence of his crooked work, and force him to let you dictate Party policies. Then you can support Danvers and everything will be sweetness and light!"

Harvey looked thoughtful, while Omega emitted a disgusted snort.

"It's an idea," Harvey said. "I'd like to do something to make up for the years that I've been running a crooked department. It'll be cleaned up from now on, of course, but I'd be really doing the city a service if I could clean house in other departments. I think…"

"How about Fowler?" asked Millicent. "He might know something you could hold over Pembroke's head. Or show you how to discover something."

Harvey was silent for several minutes. Then he slowed the car and reversed its direction.

"He might be able to help at that," he finally said. "Suppose we postpone the night's festivities until some other time. I'd like to go over some things in my files…"

"What's all this got to do with preventing the murder? It looks more like things are leading toward a murder, rather than away from one. The way Harvey used to be, he'd never have suspected that anything was wrong with the city's management. Now he's all set to monkey with things better left alone."

"Tut, tut. You are always the one who's trying to reform things. Wouldn't you like to see the taxpayer get a square deal?"

"Sure, sure. But Harvey isn't the one to start a reform. Don't forget he was a friend of mine. Went to the same schools together. I don't like to see you pushing him toward a peck of trouble."

"Don't be silly. He was due to be involved in a murder before I interfered. Therefore, anything I've done tends to influence later events so that either the murder won't happen, or Harvey won't be involved. Q.E.D. Don't forget that creek."

"Sounds logical," Mark admitted. "But it looks to me as if he's stretching out his neck."

CHAPTER IX

BIG CHIEF OMEGA

THE TELEPHONE WAS emitting a discordant jangle when Harvey let himself into his apartment. It had been ringing for some time, for he had heard it when he opened the door at the bottom of the stairs. He snatched it up now.

The voice at the other end was so excited that he didn't recognize it at first. After a minute it became coherent and he realized that it was Fowler, urging him to lock and barricade his door and wait until he arrived.

Harvey hung up, quite puzzled, but didn't bother to barricade the door. He did, however, turn out the lights and wait by the window. Nobody could enter the building without being seen from that vantage point.

Less than ten minutes passed when a taxi roared down the street and slid to a stop in front of the door. Fowler bounced out of the rear, stuffed bills into the driver's hand, and dashed for the door. Harvey let him in, whereupon he slumped in a chair to get his breath.

"What's the trouble?" Harvey, asked. "You're puffing as if you'd ran over here, instead of riding."

Fowler's respiration slowly returned to normal. "Thank God I've found you, boy. I've been chasing all over town for you. You're in grave danger!"

Harvey listened attentively as Fowler told of his interview with Pembroke, and of seeing him telephoning. "He was calling Bonzetti, sure as you're born," Fowler finished. "And it won't end with just kidnapping. Bonzetti will have to protect himself by killing you and disposing of your body in such a way that it will never be found. You've got to be on guard every minute!"

Harvey was silent for several minutes. Fowler was obviously terrified—which meant that regardless of his petty thievery and deceit in the past, he was still Harvey's friend. Nelson's scale of values underwent another sudden revision. For Fowler wasn't a man of great physical courage; yet he had knowingly risked…

"Jim," he said. "How would you like to be mayor?"

"Boy! You're delirious. Can't you understand that you're in danger? We've got to hire a bodyguard. One for me, too," he added.

"There isn't a single reason why you shouldn't be mayor. You've spent all your life in the service of this city. You've proven yourself to be a man of deep-seated integrity, and only interested in the public welfare. You've given unstintedly of your time…"

Fowler's eyes were assuming a decided poppish aspect. "Cut it out, son," he said. "There's no use being sarcastic."

"I'm talking about what the voters know to be a fact," Harvey explained. "Who knows any different?"

FOWLER LOOKED a bit sad. "Pembroke," he answered. "He knows enough to put me behind bars. Though of course I've put away enough money to pay for good lawyers. I might get out with a light sentence or maybe none at all. But that would leave me broke. And Pembroke would hand over the evidence, the minute he found I was bucking him. He may anyway, if he thinks I've spilled to you."

"Don't you have anything on him?"

"Same stuff he has on me," replied Fowler. "Graft; diversion of public funds, and all that. But he's got it on me in black and white. All I could do would be to holler, and he'd cover himself with his control of the courts. Don't forget he owns a newspaper, too. He'd whitewash himself thoroughly, saying that I was trying to get revenge with my wild accusations."

"He won't come out with that evidence," Harvey stated. "I've got something that'll stop him. And he can't white-wash himself with Uncle Sam. He's an accessory to kidnapping, and that's a federal offense, with a death penalty attached."

Fowler's eyes popped and he sputtered futilely. It was almost a minute before he could speak coherently. "Have you gone nuts?" he finally exploded. "You can't prove an accessory before the fact, when the fact hasn't happened!"

Harvey nodded. "Before and after," he stated. "Because that kidnapping is going to happen."

Fowler groaned as he saw the lines of Nelson's jaw harden, and saw what was in his mind. "Boy, boy," he wailed. "Don't do anything so foolish. Bonzetti isn't any amateur. He's thorough and efficient."

Harvey snorted. "A petty gangster," he pronounced. "I'll be ready for him. And when he kidnaps me, I'll get a confession out of him, naming Pembroke. We'll use that as a lever to elect you. Then we'll clean up the city departments until they shine."

"That's him, all right," Mark groaned. "Afraid of nothing and silly enough to buck any odds to uphold a principle. He hasn't changed a bit!"

Omega's mental voice was a bit dubious. "Hasn't changed... Oh yes he has. He's suspicious now. He used to be gullible. That's bound to change things. They won't happen as they would have."

"Of course they won't! He'll get murdered himself, instead of just being suspected of one!"

"Aw, quit worrying. I won't let anything happen to him."

Fowler shook his head miserably. "It won't work," he said. "You'll never get away, once Bonzetti gets hold of you. He's dangerous, I tell you."

Nelson smiled confidently. "He never kidnapped *me*," he said. "Listen, Jim. We'd better make sure that this really happens. As it stands now, it's merely guesswork, based on a phone call you didn't hear. Suppose we tell Pembroke we intend to run you on an independent ticket. Knowing that without the fifty-second ward he can't hope to elect Danvers, he's sure to put Bonzetti to work. That's it! Call for me about nine in the morning."

Fowler left, a scared and puzzled man. He couldn't reconcile this new Nelson with the man he had always been able to wrap around his finger with a smooth line of chatter. Now Harvey Nelson was taking the initiative, ordering *him* around!

LIGHT STREAMED through the window when Harvey awakened, and the angle indicated that the morning was well on its way. Harvey blinked and tried to get his thoughts into focus. He was looking at the ceiling while so occupied, and hence didn't notice for some minutes that he wasn't alone.

"I'm surprised at you," said a voice which he recognized immediately as being his own, which meant that it was Omega's. "Going out of your way to get us kidnapped."

"What do you mean?" Harvey began, then stopped in amazement. He had involuntarily faced the direction of the voice, and was shocked grievously as a result. For Omega seemed to have taken solid form!

Harvey looked for several seconds before he realized the truth of the situation. Omega was sitting on a chair, clad in a neat blue serge suit, fawn-colored gloves, gray socks and brown shoes. White shirt and a brown tie with yellow stripes—something Harvey had been given for Christmas—completed the outfit.

Aside from the clashing colors there was only one thing wrong with the picture—the face. The face, in fact the whole bead, was that of a ferocious Indian of the old Wild West!

Harvey stared at it for some time before he recognized it. Probably that was because the bronzed neck protruded from one of Harvey's own collars, and the feathered headdress had been broken off and the shaven scalp covered by his favorite derby; for Harvey had seen that face a thousand times. It had, in fact, stared at him inscrutably every day for the past ten years. The face belonged to a life-sized clay bust of an Indian brave, and had adorned his mantlepiece ever since he had taken this apartment.

Harvey realized that Omega's impalpable presence had

merely occupied the assorted articles of clothing, holding them—and the outraged bust—in then-proper positions. There was only one puzzling factor.

"How can you be over there?" he asked, looking behind him in the bed. "The light's casting you against the headboard."

"I've been practicing," said Omega cheerfully, getting up and walking back and forth. "I found that I'm also cast in a dozen directions by reflected ultra-violet rays. They're also light waves, you know, though quite invisible. It seems that I'm free to move about quite a bit, as long as I don't get too—*Oops!*"

The Indian's head suddenly fell through the suit of clothes and landed with a dull thud on the floor. This happened when Omega approached the opposite wall, some fifteen feet from Harvey. "Too far away," he continued. "I've been practicing walking for the last hour. Thought I'd better let you sleep."

As he talked, the clothes and the Indian head jerked themselves closer to the bed and laboriously rearranged themselves.

"Take it easy with that suit," Harvey cautioned. "It cost me fifty dollars. Say! I hope you don't intend to go around with me in that rig!"

"Why not? It's better than nothing," Omega claimed. "I felt naked before I thought this one up. Not bad, not bad."

A full-length mirror in a closet door claimed his attention. Tentatively, he bulged the place where a chest belonged, but finding that it made unsightly wrinkles and threatened the upper vest buttons, he desisted and contented himself with assuming the shape of the garments—which wasn't bad, either.

"Say, I look just like you," Omega observed.

Harvey snorted and started for the bathroom. Omega nimbly followed as Harvey tried to close the door.

"Scram!" growled Harvey, trying vainly to push him outside. "A man's entitled to some privacy."

"I can't, and you're not," Omega said, amiably. "I'll wash your back."

CHAPTER X

SNATCHED TONIGHT, GONE TOMORROW

FOWLER APPEARED, PANTING and with quivering jowls, at the stroke of nine. He looked apprehensive at the sight of Omega, who was again posing before the mirror. He had never seen an Indian, leaning forward with his eyes shaded by a gloved hand, glaring at himself in a looking glass.

But then there were a lot of things Fowler had never seen, or even imagined. He had been trying vainly, for several hours, to see himself at the head of a clean city government. He couldn't, in fact, imagine a clean city government. There was no such animal; and if such a beast were created, it would die of its own nauseating virtue.

"Friend of mine," Harvey introduced. "Been a close associate for years. Mr. Omega—Mr. Fowler."

Fowler still looked puzzled, but rallied to the occasion. He stretched forth a hand and beamed. All three chins beamed with him. His expression became a bit sickly, however, as he felt the pressure of the gloved hand. Not a feature of the redoubtable Mr. Omega changed as he turned loose a guttural: "Ugh!"

It was more than an hour later, after Harvey and Fowler had consumed hearty breakfasts—only marred by the grim countenance of Omega, who refused to eat—when Harvey's sedan stopped before a large downtown building. On the way up in the elevator Harvey coached Fowler on the way he should talk. It was necessary that Pembroke think that with Nelson out of the way, he would still be able to manipulate the fifty-second ward's vote.

THERE WAS a girl in the outer office of Pembroke's private suite. Her duty was mainly to see that nobody without an appointment gained entrance to the inner sanctum. This duty she habitually performed with utmost efficiency.

Unfortunately, however, she had never had any experience with amorous Indians. Omega, when she had shown the austere side of her nature by demanding that they return later with an appointment, decided that she needed a bit of thawing. She took one look at his expressionless face and fled, leaving the door to Pembroke's office entirely unguarded.

Pembroke's first reaction to their sudden, unannounced entry was a frown, but he quickly changed it to an affable grin when he saw Nelson. "Well, well," he said. "Harvey Nelson! Don't often see you down here. How's everything up at the fifty-second?"

He stood up, very much at ease, and shook hands heartily with Harvey Nelson.

"Fine, Mr. Pembroke," said Harvey. "Things are lined up pretty well in my ward. That's what I came down here to talk about. We think it's about time we had a little say in the matter of candidates for a change."

Pembroke sobered instantly. He looked at Fowler, who fidgeted uncomfortably. "What's on your mind?" he finally asked.

Harvey spoke calmly.

"Just this: Fowler's a pretty popular man in my ward. I've decided he ought to be mayor. We'd like the support of the Party."

Pembroke's jaw dropped perceptibly. He fumbled for a pack of cigarettes which lay on his desk, and succeeded in placing two fingers in an open inkwell. He snorted in disgust at the damage to his formerly immaculate nails. It was a full minute before he got control of himself sufficiently to compose his face into its usual affable expression.

"Fowler's a good man," he pronounced. "But the Party leaders have already decided on Danvers. We've already started our newspaper buildup. It would be a little late to change now, without jeopardizing the nomination. The reform groups are pretty strong this year, you know.

"Suppose we just let things ride and put Fowler up next election. In the meantime, that is, after this election is over, we can keep him in the public eye, so that he'll be better known when the time comes. You've got to go at these things gradually, you know."

Harvey heard him out, then shook his head vehemently. "I want Fowler nominated for this election. He'll carry my ward without any buildup. A little support from you, and we can put him in. If you don't agree, I'll run him on an independent ticket. I can elect him anyway, considering some of the things I know about Danvers."

Pembroke frowned again, and turned to inspect Omega to cover his own confusion. "Who's he?" he demanded.

"He represents the Indian vote," Harvey told him.

Omega raised his hand in what he conceived to be an Indian salute, but Pembroke was not impressed.

"Nonsense! There isn't a single Indian on the registration lists. What do you think about this, Fowler?"

Fowler fidgeted some more. He scraped his feet on the thick rug, and looked everywhere but directly at Pembroke. After a minute he answered hesitantly.

"I was against it, at first," he revealed. "You've been so set on Danvers, you know. But Nelson won't have it any other way. So I finally agreed to run. Listen, boss... Don't fly off the handle. Remember yesterday when we were talking about candidates? We never even considered me. Maybe it won't be such a bad idea after all. We always got along before and there's no reason—"

Fowler stopped, stricken dumb for the moment. Pembroke's face was the reason. It was livid with rage. The Party boss, judging by his expression, was about to have a stroke, he jumped up from his desk and began pacing the floor in short, jerky strides. This seemed to have a beneficial effect, in spite of the fact that Omega apparently decided that he should help by keeping step at his side. Eventually Pembroke stopped pacing and faced Harvey.

"Pardon me," he said, in full control of his voice. "But I was so set on electing Danvers that I couldn't see your perfectly reasonable arguments. But you're right. Fowler could be elected just as well. I'll go along with you. Danvers can wait till next election. Shake on it!"

Harvey, apparently as pleased as he should be, shook hands with the Party boss. Fowler did likewise, beaming all over his face. Omega said, "Ugh!" and snatched Pembroke's cigarette from his mouth and tried to puff it. He didn't do so well, but Harvey managed to cover him up by distracting Pembroke's attention.

"He's not used to cigarettes," said Harvey. "But he left his peace pipe home."

Omega said, "Ugh!" again.

The three visitors left on that happy note, with Pembroke smilingly bidding them goodbye and assuring them that he'd get the publicity wheels in motion to push Fowler for mayor.

"I don't like it," said Fowler, climbing into the back of Harvey's car. "He didn't make near the fuss I expected him to. He's got something up his sleeve."

"Sure he has," agreed Harvey. "You missed the point, Jim. He's going to announce the candidacy of Danvers in the next edition of the sheet. And I'll be kidnapped before tomorrow!"

CHAPTER XI

OMEGA'S SLIPPING

OMEGA LEAPED INTO the driver's seat, gripped the wheel and looked stonily ahead. Harvey, on the point of disputing the act, changed his mind with the thought that if he objected too strenuously, Omega would only desert his suit of clothes and take over the driving anyway.

And being a little troubled mentally, he didn't feel up to the ordeal of wrestling and driving at the same time.

The car started off with a roar, Omega skillfully missing a trolley car and two trucks, all three of which seemed bent on the sedan's annihilation. Harvey let out a groan and began to wish he hadn't given up without an argument.

Fowler shook his head in bafflement. "I thought that was all over," he said. "With Pembroke agreeing…"

"You missed the point," Harvey repeated. "Pembroke only pretended to accept my ultimatum. Your own words, which sounded vacillating to him, convinced him that you'd toe the line, with me out of the way, and do all you could to insure the fifty-second ward voting the right way. That was the idea of the visit. I didn't expect him to pretend to agree, but the result will be the same. Bonzetti will probably visit my flat tonight. And I'll be ready for him."

"I don't like it," Fowler proclaimed. "Those gangsters might decide to—*Hey!*"

Next on the program was a matter which required no planning, no rehearsal. It was one of those things which just happen, without human regulation of any kind. The sedan was rolling at quite a moderate pace, something less than fifty, when suddenly a tire blew out.

It was a front tire, the right one, and Omega had some trouble with the wheel. So much, in fact, that he gave up the job and jumped into the back of the car, holding his gloves over his clay head. He whimpered pitifully as the car mounted the curb and jolted to a stop against a tree, removing quite a bit of bark and bending the bumper badly.

HARVEY SWORE hugely as he pushed Omega off his lap. Fowler quivered with indignation as Omega landed on his insteps. He glared at Harvey.

"I don't admire the courage of your red-skinned friend in the face of an emergency!" he said, with a certain cutting pointedness.

"Tell him how fragile I am," whined Omega.

"I thought Indians were a hardy race, rugged and fearless," objected Fowler.

"Not his tribe," said Harvey. "They're very delicate, and afraid of their own shadows. Few, in fact, ever reach maturity."

"You said it," Omega confirmed. "I'm the only one who ever grew up."

"That's impossible!" intruded a new voice. "I suppose your mother was an infant when you were born. And your father— Say, who was driving this car?"

Harvey groaned as he saw the gray of a state police uniform.

"Very pretty uniform," Omega remarked. "Ugh!"

"Don't change the subject," said the cop, severely. "Who was driving this car? I've been following you for a mile, and I never saw such screwy driving in my life. Who's the guilty man?"

Harvey was trying to make up his mind whether to point out Omega as the guilty one, or to say that he'd been piloting the car himself, when suddenly he stiffened at the sight of something decidedly unusual across the street. Four men were

Omega merely said, "Aaahh!" and collapsed;
the clothes dummy and clothes he'd been
holding together fell to the sidewalk

running out of the wide doorway of a bank and heading for a car parked at the curb. Each carried a satchel which seemed to be heavily loaded.

"Look!" he cried, and swung open the car door.

"No you don't!" the policeman began; then suddenly stopped at the sound of a shot.

A bank guard had appeared at the door and opened fire. Simultaneously with the shot, the bandit car darted away from the curb, only to crash into the side of a trolley, which stopped, effectively blocking the getaway. The bandits piled out and one of them snapped a shot at the bank guard. He fell heavily, hit in the thigh.

HARVEY LEAPED from the car, intent on tackling the rearmost of the bandits from behind. He could have done so had not the state policeman opened fire at that moment. One of the bandits went down, spilling his satchel, and the others turned, firing as they sighted the new enemy.

Omega probably saved Harvey's life at that instant; for two of the bandits were firing directly toward him. Omega, apparently afraid of being left behind, had dashed across the street and tried to halt Harvey, stepping in front of him in the process. He was just in time to stop a couple of bullets with his clay head.

This infuriated him, for both entered his high-bridged nose, damaging it beyond repair. Instead of trying to stop Harvey, he decided to take a hand. A flying tackle, which would have put him on that year's All-American had he been playing for Carlisle, brought down one of the bandits.

The impact spoiled the shape of Omega's derby, but it did much greater damage to the bandit. His breath left with a finality which indicated that he was permanently out of the battle. A gun fell from limp fingers and Harvey snatched it up.

The state cop had just winged his second man as Harvey returned the fire of the remaining gunman. The bandit's bullet went wide of its mark, mainly because he was trying to run and shoot at the same time. Harvey, on the other hand, stood still, slightly crouched, and fired just once. The bandit dropped forward on his face.

"Nice work," said the cop, picking up one of the satchels of loot. "Say, your friend must have been hit!"

Harvey turned to see Omega covering his shattered nose with both gloves. He was moaning softly, as if in pain.

"You better get him to a hospital," said the cop. "He looks bad. Gimme your names first. There might be a reward out for those guys. You two sure earned a share of it—"

Omega was hunched over, and was covering his damaged features completely, which gave Harvey an idea. The policeman, who was fortified by the name of O'Reilly, took down the information Harvey gave him. Two city cops arrived at that moment and took charge of the disabled bandits, one of whom was already qualified for entry into the nether regions. O'Reilly disappeared into the bank, carrying the two heavy satchels. Harvey took Omega's arm and guided him across the street.

"You double-crosser!" growled Omega, taking his gloves away from the damaged proboscis.

Harvey chuckled for a moment and then laughed.

"The conniving scoundrel didn't give me any credit! Omega growled to Fowler.

"Why should I?" asked Harvey, chuckling some more. "You didn't risk anything. Bullets can't hurt you. And besides you wouldn't have come along if you weren't afraid I'd get hit, and thereby put an end to you."

"I don't get it," said Fowler.

Omega grunted. "He gave his own name when the cop asked for it, and then when he asked who I was, he said James Fowler!"

"It won't hurt being a hero on election day," Harvey explained. "And the cop didn't get a good look at Omega until it was all over. And then he had his face covered. The reporters will give you a big write-up, and the thing will be mentioned every time the papers carry a campaign story."

HARVEY WAS right. In less than an hour the reporters caught up with them. They were waiting, in fact, when Harvey and Fowler arrived at the second-floor flat after putting the damaged car in a nearby garage.

Omega, fortunately, had decided to vacate his human form, because of the damaged face. He had done it in the car, and Harvey's borrowed suit of clothes had collapsed in a heap.

Fowler's expression as he faced the reporters gave evidence of the shock he had received when Harvey had explained the true nature of his "close associate." It lent a degree of authenticity to Harvey's description of the terrific battle which the "future mayor of this city" had given. Cameras clicked and everybody was happy. Except, perhaps, Mr. Fowler.

"Wait'll that cop sees my picture," he groaned, after they were inside.

"He won't know the difference," Harvey assured. "Quit worrying. You ought to be happy. We've announced your candidacy, and at the same time the voters will read of your heroic deed and realize that you are a man who puts his duty above all else, even his personal safety. It's the biggest thing that—"

He stopped at the look on Fowler's face. It expressed something that even that versatile physiognomy seldom contained. There was a sadness there, but also a look of shame, as if Fowler was suddenly becoming aware that there was much wanting in his character.

"Look, Harvey," he pleaded. "Let's drop the whole thing and take my hat out of the ring. Let's go tell Pembroke you've decided to back Danvers... All right. All right. But then get a bodyguard and protect yourself against Bonzetti. I can't let you take this risk."

It was Fowler's turn to lapse into silence. Harvey's face had told him there wasn't any sense in arguing. He left, shaking his head miserably.

> *"I'm slipping!"*
> *"I've known that for years," said Mark, calmly.*

"*I mean I can't seem to stay in one place in time! Look!*"

Mark became suddenly alarmed. He was looking at Fowler as he closed the door behind him, when the door suddenly ceased to exist! Instead he looked out on a battlefield, a torn shambles of shell holes and twisted barbed wire.

But only for a second. The scene changed to one of tranquility almost immediately. Once more he was looking at the muddy creek bed from which the water had diverted. He looked behind him and saw the new creek as it wound its way parallel to the old.

"*What's the idea?*" *he asked.* "*We're back where we started.*"

"*I know. I told you it took an effort to hold myself that far back in time. We'll have to go back again, if you want to continue interfering in people's normal lives.*"

"*Of course I do! You've got to go back. Harvey's liable to be kidnapped while we're gone.*"

"*Don't worry about that. If he is, we'll just jump further back to where he isn't... Say! Look at that!*"

Startled, Mark looked further up the creek, to the point where Omega had started his ravine. The water was flowing back into the old creek bed!

Mark turned on Omega.

"*Do you see what that means?*" *he yelled.* "*You didn't change history! The creek's back where it started! And silt will fill up the ravine you cut!*"

"*That was an accident,*" *Omega said, dubiously.* "*But maybe we'd better go back and see what happens to Nelson. This might...*"

CHAPTER XII

THE ETHICS OF MILLY

HARVEY MADE FOR his bathroom and took a satisfying shower. He wasn't bothered by Omega this time. In fact, Omega hadn't bothered him all afternoon.

After Fowler had left, Harvey had repaired the damage to his clothes, and gone immediately to his office. He had been busy all afternoon helping straighten out the mess caused by the fire. A few records had been salvaged, but nothing of any great use to him. He was really more of a nuisance than anything, considering that the janitors were cleaning very efficiently until he arrived. But Harvey had thought it best to be present in his usual haunts, to make things easier for Bonzetti.

He didn't want the gangster to have any trouble finding him. He really didn't expect the kidnapping to occur in the daytime, or indeed at any time when it could be witnessed; for Pembroke would probably want to concoct a story that he had left town of his own accord and for his own reasons. Otherwise it would be hard to control the fifty-second ward.

With this thought in mind, as the afternoon waned, Harvey had decided to make good his promise to Millicent to resume the celebration of the night before. Bonzetti wouldn't strike, he had decided, until the small hours of the morning, when everybody was asleep in Harvey's neighborhood. And Harvey would make sure he was home by then.

Secretly he hoped that Omega would wake up by the time Bonzetti arrived; his help would be welcome. But in the meantime he didn't want Omega around. Harvey decided to keep his mind rigidly away from thoughts concerning him, half afraid a mere thought would return him to consciousness.

By keeping his mind strictly occupied with the subject of the coming campaign while he bathed and dressed, he managed to forget completely about that disconcerting character.

It didn't, however, do a bit of good. An hour later, while passing a haberdashery shop, he felt a sudden dig in the ribs.

"Inside!" hissed Omega. "There's a few things I need. You keep quiet. I'll do the talking."

Harvey heaved a resigned sigh, and entered the store. A smiling clerk greeted him. Harvey nodded, but didn't open his mouth.

"There's a gray hat in the window, sitting on the head of a good-looking dummy," said Omega. "Bring in the whole works."

For a second or two the clerk looked at Harvey, who hadn't moved his lips, before he decided to obey. Then he reached in the show window and brought out the desired articles. The dummy was handsome, with a cleancut jaw and twinkling eyes. It looked straight in front, but had that quality—shared by most portraits—of appearing to look sideways if one regarded it from an angle.

"The hat isn't a very good fit," Omega said.

"But you haven't tried it on," the clerk reminded.

"I mean it doesn't fit the dummy," Omega said. "Get one just like it, but a size or two smaller. Make it fit the dummy pretty tight."

The clerk look mystified, but removed the gray hat from the handsome clay head, and went toward the back of the store. Omega was probably very gratified to note that the dummy was crowned by a shock of wavy dark brown hair. The clerk returned and fitted a new hat over the wavy hair. This one was snug. He looked up expectantly.

"Good! I'll take it," Omega said. "Boy, will I wow the dames! How much?"

The clerk looked startled. "Five for the hat," he said, hesitantly. "Five more for the dummy, if that's what you want."

"Who's a dummy?" roared Omega, his voice coming from the clay head.

"Just practicing a ventriloquism act," Harvey explained, smiling.

The clerk took the ten-dollar bill and shook his head as Harvey walked out of the store with his purchase under his arm.

"Don't do things like that!" Harvey raged, mentally. "Keep it up and we'll be locked up in a booby hatch."

"Well then, don't try to sneak out and have fun while I'm asleep. Go on home now and give me a chance to wrap that swell head up in some clothes. Then we'll go out together."

MILLICENT, LOOKING her loveliest, quite took Harvey's breath away when he and Omega stopped for her. This condition didn't hold true for his shadow. Not having any breath to lose, he didn't lose it. He walked right past Harvey and attempted to embrace her.

Millicent, being a girl of some constancy, gave him a straight-arm which almost took his head off. Only the fact that Harvey's collar was a bit tight on the masculine clay neck saved that masterpiece of the window-display manufacturer's art.

Omega was a bit sulky after that. He refused to eat a bite of the excellent meal which Harvey ordered in one of the city's leading restaurants. Nor did he say a single word.

As a matter of fact he was trying most mightily to make his clay visage scowl; but such was the hardness and inflexibility of the substance of which it was composed, that it wouldn't even frown. His affable, good-natured expression was immovably fixed. Several times, in an effort to catch it off guard, he suddenly ceased trying to frown and attempted a sneer. The face still refused to cooperate.

"Do you really think everything will be all right?" Millicent asked. "About Fowler for mayor, I mean."

Harvey frowned. "Oh... You've seen the papers!"

Harvey suddenly realized that he would have to dissemble—though doing it wouldn't be easy for him. Obviously he couldn't tell Millicent that he expected to be kidnapped some time before tomorrow morning. She wouldn't approve of it. So he'd have to do a bit of evading.

Abruptly he realized that perhaps he'd made a mistake in announcing Fowler's candidacy so soon. Maybe Pembroke wouldn't order any kidnapping after all. Maybe he'd decide that as long as the afternoon papers had come out with the story of Fowler's hat in the ring, it might be best to go along, knowing that he could control Fowler, rather than risk a rumor of dissension in the party ranks.

Then where would he, Harvey Nelson, be? Somewhere on the lee side of the eight ball, he guessed.

"How did you ever get Pembroke to agree to do it?" asked Milly.

"I demanded it. And as far as Pembroke is concerned, Fowler is as good a stooge as Danvers. He expects to be able to dictate to him."

"But how can you prevent..."

Harvey frowned. "That's the only trouble right now. I've got to get something on Pembroke, to hold over his head. There's no other way to insure the city a clean administration."

Harvey once more became lost in thought. He wasn't dissembling at all. He'd told the truth. He did have to get something on Pembroke. It wasn't at all certain that any kidnapping would be perpetrated on his person. He'd just have to assume that there wouldn't, and go to work from scratch. The darned thing was getting more complicated by the minute. He almost wished...

"HE'S BEEN a stooge all his life," Omega muttered. "Now he's going to pass up his chance to get even with that pack of crooks."

"What do you mean?" asked Millicent.

Omega, with his expressionless clothing-store-dummy
face, sat at the bar and watched them in the mirror.
Danvers and the blonde had minds worth reading

"He's going to give the taxpayer a break, instead of cleaning up," Omega growled. "He could take all the gravy himself,
maybe cutting Fowler in for a small percentage. But no. Little
Rollo has to give the taxpayer a break. He's dumb. He don't even
understand the simplest principles behind the democratic form
of government."

"Tell me about them," requested Millicent, apparently
intensely interested.

"It's simple," said Omega. "In a monarchy, one big shot robs
the citizens, only splitting a very small percentage with his
stooges, called nobles. In a democracy things are different. There
is a more equitable distribution of the swag. All the big party
workers take a slice, so that no one man has the sole privilege
of robbing the people.

"But this gent cuts himself right out of the gravy. He don't
think the citizens should be robbed at all! It's unprecedented,
that's what it is. He ought to be stopped. First thing you know
there'll be a revolution."

Millicent looked troubled. "Do you think that's best, Harvey?" she asked. "After all, we don't want a revolution."

Harvey got red in the face and glared at Omega. "Yes we do," he claimed. "Once the people realize that the city government can be run on a greatly reduced budget, they won't stand for an increase when Jim's term of office is over. It'll be a revolution, all right. A complete change from the corruption which has thrived in the past."

Omega snorted. "So you think it'll last, do you? You're wrong. It'll last just as long as you do. As soon as you're voted out, the gang will take over again. Maybe not the same gang, of course. But the budget will increase just the same. It'll happen by degrees, so slow that the people won't notice, but it'll finally get back to where it is now.

"There's a natural law controlling it. A law just as binding as the law of gravitation. It's called: All the Traffic Will Bear. When taxes reach that point, then the boys slow down, if they're smart. If they're too greedy, then they get kicked out and the cycle starts all over again.

"And listen, Boy Scout—the same thing happens with any form of government, not just the democratic. Your history books are full of it. The taxpayer is the sucker, and there's always somebody to take him. So why bat your head against a stone wall?"

Harvey nodded. "That's all very true," he admitted. "But you take the wrong attitude, and therefore you forget one little item: your vanishing point, All the Traffic Will Bear, is getting smaller and smaller. The people are slowly getting smarter, and consequently harder to rob. The Fowler administration will leave the people of this city a little smarter than they were before. An honest administration will show them approximately what it costs to run the city. Result? The next crooked gang to take over won't be able to steal quite as much as if there had never been a Fowler administration."

Omega scratched at a chin which couldn't possibly itch. "Too fanciful," he finally commented.

"It's all in the attitude," Harvey amplified. "The proper attitude is that each step in the right direction is a means toward realizing the desired end, that of absolutely clean government, existing for the people and not for itself."

"And what's it get you?" retorted Omega. "Glory?"

Millicent decided to take a hand. "What does the other attitude get Pembroke?" she countered. "He's trembling in his boots, scared to death that his crooked work will be exposed. He doesn't have the respect of any man. Do you want Harvey to be in that position?"

Harvey regarded her quizzically. "Whose side are you on?" he asked. "One minute graft is all right if it gets you a honeymoon in Bermuda. Next…"

"Your side, darling," Said Millicent sweetly. "If you want graft, I'll be corrupt. If you don't, I'll join a Sunday school, or something. If you want gambling and vice, I'll open a—"

"Okay," said Harvey, hastily. "That covers the subject. In fact, I think we'd better go see Patelli, right now. I'm going to need some help."

CHAPTER XIII

INSIDE A BLONDE'S MIND

INSIDE THE DOOR of Club Patelli Harvey was stopped short. Two young men, immaculately dressed, stepped in front of him, scowling but sober. Harvey recognized them after a second, though they looked slightly different than they had when he last saw them.

"We want to know," said the foremost, slightly belligerent, "what you pulled on us last night."

"Why nothing. Nothing at all," Harvey answered, piloting Millicent past them.

"Oh yes you did," the other persisted. "You see we can't usually remember what happens when we get drunk, but this morning we both seem to remember the same thing—that you made your hat sail through the air by lifting your left eyebrow. That's silly!"

At the last word, spoken with such vehemence, Harvey's eyebrows lifted involuntarily. His hat, and Omega's as well, rose in the air and floated gently into the hands of the waiting wardrobe girl.

"You lifted both eyebrows!" accused the first young man. "You're trying to confuse us!"

"You confuse easy," Harvey stated. "Two hats, two eyebrows. Very simple."

The two stood dumbfounded as Harvey and his companions followed the headwaiter to a choice table. Then, after exchanging quick glances, they proceeded furtively to a nearby table and sat down. The shorter of the two cleverly removed a "reserved" sign and concealed it in a flower vase.

"Ask Mr. Patelli if he'll join us when he gets a chance," Harvey requested, handing the headwaiter a folded bill.

Mr. Patelli, it seemed, made his own chances. He excused himself from the company of a beautiful woman and a prosperous-appearing, middle-aged man, as soon as the headwaiter spoke to him. He was all smiles as he sat down at Harvey's table. He shook hand with "Mr. Omega" and beamed affably. Then he signaled a waiter and ordered drinks.

"I thought I was going to have some fun needling Danvers, over at the bar," he said. "About your announcement in the afternoon papers, you know. But he didn't needle so good."

"How did he like the idea of Fowler for mayor?" Harvey asked.

"I don't know," Patelli said. "He was smart enough not to show he was mad. Just said what a good man Fowler is, and that he thought the party had made a wise choice." He paused. "That came as a big surprise to me," he added. "I thought they were already building Danvers up for the job."

Harvey nodded. "It was my work," he admitted. "Pembroke went along when he saw that I could lick him. He double-crossed Danvers without turning a hair. Which gives you a good idea what might happen in your own case."

Patelli frowned. "I don't get it," he admitted.

HARVEY DOWNED his drink with a quick gesture. "You told me last night that Pembroke taxed you out of business when you had a gambling joint," he reminded. "You also mentioned the fact that if the reform bunch got in, they could easily shorten your hours to the point where the profit would disappear. That's why you wanted to know which way the primaries would go."

"Yeah. I asked all the big shots, before I asked you. They all said they couldn't be sure until you said which way the fifty-second would vote."

"Then Pembroke knows what harm the reform crowd could

do if they shortened your hours," Harvey said. "What's to prevent him from telling you that he intends to do the same thing unless all the night-club operators hand over a substantial donation to the party fund? He's greedy, you know. He's bled everybody he can, up to the present."

Patelli frowned. "You think he might do that?" he asked, anxiously. "I've already passed up a chance at the best spot on the edge of town. You said—"

"I merely said that I thought you'd do better to stay in town," Harvey reminded. "I still do. We're putting in a party man, Fowler. He won't do any of the things the reform gang would be sure to do. But Pembroke still controls the party. Now suppose we managed to displace him?"

"Could that be done?"

"It's possible," said Harvey. "If we could prove something on him, he'd have to step down to keep us quiet. Patelli, you said you once handed over some graft to Pembroke, didn't you?"

Patelli nodded.

"Do you know any others? Men who are now engaged in legitimate business?"

Patelli grinned. "I gotcha," he said. "Sure. I know half a dozen. Two ran speakeasies during prohibition, and a couple were in the same racket as me. There's another I know used to be a numbers banker and—" Patelli's face suddenly fell.

"What now?" asked Harvey.

"I just happened to remember. We never had any dealings with Pembroke direct. Always it was donations to the party fund, like you said."

Omega grunted. "What's the difference?" he said. "Six to one. You can say you gave it to him, can't you? You kept records, didn't you?"

Patelli's eyes gleamed. "I'll have to round up the boys," he said. "We'll figure something out. But wait a minute! How do we know Fowler won't pull something? He was always hand in glove with Pembroke."

Harvey grinned. "He isn't now. Fowler will do as I advise. Is that enough?"

"Mr. Nelson," said Patelli, "the boys all know about you. If you say Fowler will leave us alone, we're for Fowler."

Millicent puckered up her lips and made a very unladylike sound, aiming it in Omega's direction. "Yaah," she said. "See what an honest man can do? Pembroke couldn't get anybody to trust him even if he paid them."

Omega's amiable expression didn't change to one of chagrin, though he tried hard enough. "It won't help much," he said pessimistically.

THE TWO young men at the adjoining table eyed Patelli suspiciously as he left Harvey's table with such a purposeful stride. Then their attention reverted to Harvey, who noticed them at that moment. He was embarrassed at the fixity of their gazes.

They looked at him unblinkingly, evidently determined not to miss his slightest move. A bottle, already far from full, stood between them within reach of either. And from the look of it, both were reaching frequently.

"We're being watched," Harvey remarked. "Incidentally, how did you manage to do that hat trick without using your hands?"

"Simple," Omega claimed. "I'm not all inside this suit, you know. I extend in all directions around you, wherever there's a light on the other side. Even ultraviolet and infra red, which you can't even see. I'm a very remarkable—What are you looking at?" The last was directed to Millicent, who was regarding him calculatingly.

"You," she said, quietly. "I heard of drowning a shadow, once. I think we'll try it on you. No hard feelings, of course."

"You'll have to drown Harvey," said Omega, with a sneer in his voice, though his face was pleasant enough.

"She has the right idea, though," agreed Harvey. "Look—if you were going to commit suicide, how would you go about it?"

Omega chuckled malevolently. "I'd shoot you," he answered.

Millicent frowned prettily. "That won't do," she said, apparently weighing the suggestion carefully. "But I think there might be a way of shooting you. The idea just occurred to me—"

"Won't work," Omega interrupted. "But has it occurred to either of you that Danvers might know something incriminating about Pembroke? He's the party treasurer, isn't he?"

Harvey started. "And you can read minds! Let's go!"

Millicent bit her lip and followed that by finishing her drink with a very unladylike gulp, as her companions abruptly deserted her and made for the bar.

"Head for that space down toward this end of the bar," Omega said. "There's a light that'll cast me in the right direction."

Harvey stopped at the space indicated. He ordered two Scotch-and-seltzers. Danvers, in the company of a shapely blonde who was smiling at him bewitchingly, was about ten feet from him, and clearly visible in the mirror behind the bar.

"What are they talking about?" he asked.

"Quiet! I'm working on the dame. Oh boy, oh boy! Say, you ought to cultivate her acquaintance. But if you do, keep your hand on your wallet."

"I'm not fickle," Harvey thought. "Start to work on Danvers."

For a long minute Omega said nothing, either aloud or in Harvey's brain. He just looked pleasantly at himself in the mirror. Harvey also regarded the mirror as he finished his own drink and started on Omega's. He couldn't hear anything that was said. The humming babble of nearer voices prevented that.

"Let's go," said Omega.

Harvey downed the remainder of the drink and headed back to the table. "What did you learn?" he asked.

"Wait'll we get back," said Omega, shortly.

"Did you notice who the blonde was?"

"I never forget a figure," Mark answered. "She's still alive, it seems. Do you suppose…"

"Can't tell," Omega answered. "We may have prevented her

murder, at that. It might tie in somewhere with what we've done.
Then again, maybe, it just hasn't happened yet."

"When was she killed?" Mark inquired. "Can't you place it?"

"I can't identify anything in its relation to things we've changed,"
Omega answered, with a degree of asperity. "I'm not used to this! I've
got no power. I'll be glad when we return to the present."

MILLICENT LOOKED expectant but refrained from asking
questions. Harvey was just as curious, but he also said nothing.
Both looked at Omega, who seemed to be enjoying himself,
keeping them on edge. The band was playing a discordant jitter-
bug number, and he was apparently absorbed in the ear-split-
ting cacophony. By the time he decided to speak, Harvey was
fingering a table knife and seemed about to try its effectiveness
on Omega's clay throat.

"Open up, you animated dummy," threatened Harvey, "before
I tear off that stone head of yours and throw it in your face."

"It's a very peculiar situation," said Omega, ignoring the
outburst. Then he seemed to forget what he was going to say,
and became lost in the raucous efforts of the band.

"Go ahead, darling," advised Millicent. "Stab him. He might
have a vital organ if you hit the right place."

"Might ruin my suit," muttered Harvey.

"It seems," mused Omega, "that Danvers is in a bad spot. He
made a list of last year's important contributions to the party
fund, at Pembroke's request, and lost it!"

Harvey grunted. "How's that put him in bad?" he asked. "He
can make another list. I can get that information, myself."

"It also seems that along with the list were two other papers,"
Omega continued imperturbably. "These contained the itemized
expenditures for the year. One paper wasn't the same as the other,
but the totals of both agreed with the total of the contributions."

Harvey looked suddenly thoughtful. "I get it!" he suddenly
erupted. "One was the list of expenditures which everybody
sees, including advertising, rentals, etcetera. The other was a list

revealing how the money was actually spent. Rentals, advertising, etcetera were much less than on the other list. Right?"

"Right," said Omega. "The difference went to Pembroke mainly, though there were a few other beneficiaries—minor ones who couldn't be given city jobs to pay for their services."

There was a long silence, only punctuated by screaming blasts from the orchestra trumpet, which fondly believed it was playing music.

"Let's hear the rest," said Harvey, quietly. "Who's the blonde with the curves?"

"Oh, so you noticed that!" said Millicent, somewhat vexed. "I suppose you'd—"

Harvey stopped her with a finger to his lips. "I didn't say I liked 'em," he reminded. "Only a blind man could miss them."

"Not even a blind man," said Millicent. "If he knew his Braille…"

"Her name's Dolly Patterson," Omega revealed. "She copped the lists—"

AT THIS point Omega's recital of the facts gleaned by his mind-reading was interrupted by the arrival of Joe Patelli. He grasped the back of an unoccupied chair and slid it between Harvey and Omega.

"I got in touch with the boys," he informed. "They all kept records of their payments. They're willing to hand them over, if they're of any use to you. But the fools want to keep out of it personally. They're so darned respectable now that they don't want any publicity if they can get out of it. They figure you might be able to use their records to make Pembroke play ball, just by threatening to make them public."

Harvey nodded. "It'll help," he said. "Get hold of them as soon as you can, will you?"

"By midnight," Patelli promised. "I'll start now."

He left the table and Harvey turned to Omega. "Get back to

your story," he requested. "What does Dolly Patterson intend to do with those lists?"

Omega hesitated. "I must have missed that," he admitted. "You told me to get to work on Danvers, and I didn't get that far into her mind. I suppose she figures on selling them back to Danvers—or maybe Pembroke."

Harvey abruptly shoved himself away from the table. "It doesn't matter anyway," he said. "I've got to get hold of..."

"Harvey Nelson!" Millicent interrupted, with fire in her eye. "Keep away from that bulgy woman!"

"Can't," he said. "I've got to get my hands on those lists! Before she has a chance to—"

"Harvey Nelson," said Millicent, quietly. "You stay away from that over-upholstered—"

Omega cut her short. "We're too late," he said. "She and Danvers have gone."

CHAPTER XIV

THE GREAT DARKNESS

THE DOORMAN HAD little to offer in the way of information, except for the fact that Danvers and the blonde had taken a cab. He had held the door for them, but hadn't heard Danvers give an address. In fact, he was almost sure that no address had been given.

"If you really want to find out," he suggested, "just wait here a while. The driver will come back. That is, unless he gets another fare before he returns."

"Omega," muttered Harvey. "Did you happen to learn the lady's address while you were reading her mind?"

Omega didn't answer for several seconds. When he did, he merely said: "Aaaah…" and then punctuated the remark by collapsing limply to the sidewalk. The clay dummy landed with a dull thud amidst the crumpled wearing apparel. It cocked itself sideways and smiled pleasantly at no one in particular.

"He's fainted!" cried Millicent.

"He went to sleep," corrected Harvey, gathering up the debris. "Or whatever it is he does in place of sleep. There's nothing to do but wait for that driver."

"What happened to your friend?" asked the doorman, looking a bit startled.

"Huh… Oh, him?" Harvey hesitated. "He was in a hurry. Didn't realize how fast he is, I guess."

FAIRVIEW ARMS was quite a hotel. More stories high than

Harvey cared to crane his neck to see, it was pretentious and obviously expensive. Dolly, it appeared, did well for herself.

The desk clerk supplied the number of her suite. Also the information that she had come in about an hour ago and had been escorted to the elevator by a prosperous-looking, middle-aged man who had then left the place by the front entrance.

"That's a break," said Harvey, in the elevator. "I was wondering how I'd get rid of Danvers."

"What are you going to do?" Millicent asked. "Buy those lists?"

"Nothing else to do. Omega is asleep or something. I've tried calling his name, mentally, but he doesn't answer."

Dolly's suite was at the end of the corridor on the twelfth floor. Harvey knocked at the door. There wasn't any answer, and he knocked again, this time a little harder. The ornamental brass knocker banged loudly enough to wake the lady within, if she had gone to bed already. But she didn't answer, nevertheless.

"Maybe she went out again," Harvey said. "The room clerk might have missed her."

Millicent nodded, and absently tried the knob. Surprisingly the door opened. She peered inside as Harvey looked over her shoulder. Then she stepped back with a gasp. At the same instant Harvey cursed softly and pushed her inside, closing the door quietly behind him.

Millicent's hand was over her mouth to stifle a scream and her eyes were wide with horror as she took in the scene before her.

Mark saw Omega—clothes, dummy, shoes and all—collapse in a heap. Then for a brief instant there was a rapidly changing series of scenes and thousands of years sped haltingly past. He sensed the struggle Omega was putting up to stay in one place, and realized that he was losing miserably. Finally both of them stopped at the edge of the artificial creek-bed.

Omega let out a hollow groan. Mark instantly saw the reason. For the ravine was completely dry, and the portion above the fallen tree had filled up with silt, as Mark had predicted.

Omega turned loose a string of profanity culled from a thousand languages, both terrestrial and otherwise. "I keep getting weaker every minute I stay in the past," he complained. "Why I was even beginning to merge with Harvey!"

"Nonsense!" Mark derided. "You, who can move mountains…"

"I tell you I was," Omega insisted. "I wasn't fooling when I told Harvey to stand at the bar so that his shadow would be cast in the right direction. It was so! I can't move without him, back there.

"Mark, you have no idea of the power of thought. Harvey implicitly believes I'm his shadow—which tends to make it true. He believes it, and I am continually fostering the belief. It gets strong. Fowler and Milly, both believing the same yarn, strengthen it even more. Milly especially has been giving me a lot of thought."

"But you have to go back," Mark said, beginning to grow alarmed. "It begins to look as if you haven't changed history very much, judging by that creek. But you can influence people's minds. You've got to go back! And when that murder happens, you've got to take the suspicion out of that cop's mind."

Omega didn't answer immediately. Mark was beginning to think he didn't intend to, when he abruptly felt faint and things went black. It lightened almost immediately, and he found himself looking at the very same scene he had encountered on his first journey back to the twentieth century. There, beneath him, was the curvaceous blonde, with her throat thoroughly cut.

"This is where we came in," he remarked.

"No, it isn't," Omega denied. "Look around."

Mark did. He saw Harvey Nelson quietly closing the door. Milly was staring, horrified, at the corpse. But there wasn't a sign of a cop or a medical examiner.

"We'll stay," Omega said. "We haven't missed much. I'm afraid to try again, anyhow. Too weak… Mark! I'm merging again!"

CHAPTER XV

HOW DO YOU KILL A SHADOW?

"**CALL THE ROOM** clerk," Harvey said. "Tell him to phone the police immediately. I'm going to take a quick look around. Those lists may be in this room!"

Millicent got control of herself sufficiently to obey, then turned from the phone to help him. But Harvey didn't need any help; he was standing in the middle of the room looking helplessly around him. And then Millicent saw what, in the shock of finding the body, just hadn't registered before—the room had already been ransacked!

It was obvious that the desk, the most likely place to look, had been searched first. Its contents hadn't been scattered so much; obviously the searcher had not been in a great hurry when he searched it.

The bedroom, however, revealed that the searcher had been getting panicky. He had emptied the bureau drawers on the bed, then had pulled the mattress on the floor and searched it, letting the stuff fall where it might. And the bathroom—with contents of the medicine case scattered everywhere—showed that the searcher had become positively frantic toward the end.

And it all added up to one thing: whoever had made that search hadn't found what he was looking for—in other words, the lists that Danvers had lost and wanted back. Harvey was willing to bet on that; for it was the desk that had been searched first. His eyes strayed to the inert form of Dolly Patterson. There was the answer! The one place the murderer hadn't looked.

Millicent gasped as she saw Harvey carefully step to the side of the body, avoiding the crimson stains, and bend over it. He appeared to ponder for a brief instant; then he began to explore the tops of the stockings. At length he stood up again; Millicent watched him with narrowed eyes as he examined the three tightly-folded papers he now held.

"Knew right where to go!" she observed rather tartly.

Harvey had no chance to answer, for at that moment a step sounded outside the door. It opened and three men came in, the foremost being a large, ruddy-faced individual who looked very much like a policeman, but happened to be the medical examiner. He immediately proved it by examining the body.

The second—small, dapper and sporting a close-clipped mustache across his upper lip—looked very much like a professional man, but was actually a lieutenant in the homicide squad. The third was O'Reilly, of the state police, in civilian clothes.

"Hiya, Mr. Nelson," said O'Reilly. "Fancy meeting—"

"Shut up!" said the dapper man. "I told you to keep quiet if you want to come along. You know these people?"

"How can I answer and shut up, too?" demanded O'Reilly.

"Answer first, shut up afterward," said the smaller man. "Who are they?"

O'Reilly introduced Nelson, sulkily. The lieutenant, he said, was named Schwartz.

"Now shut up," advised Lieutenant Schwartz. He changed his scowl to a grin, aimed at Harvey. "These state coppers are always butting in, Mr. Nelson. Got to put them in their place. That your wife?"

"Not yet," said Harvey, and introduce Millicent.

"How'd it happen?" asked Schwartz next.

"Can't say," answered Harvey. "I think the room clerk will tell you we called him as soon as we got up here."

"He already did," said Schwartz. "Just thought I'd ask. What d'ya say, doc?"

THE BEEFY medical man groaned slightly as he rose to his feet. "Struck over the head and knocked unconscious," he said musingly. "Died a few minutes later."

Schwartz looked astounded. "Doc," he pleaded. "Didn't you notice she had her throat cut? Or did she bite herself as she fell?"

"Fractured skull," said the medical man, slowly. "That's what she died of. Struck from behind. Landed on her face, judging from that bruise on her cheek. Later she was turned over and her throat cut. That blood seeped out; it wasn't pumped out by a heart which was still beating. The quantity, as well as the distribution, proves that. If she'd been alive when the throat was cut, the blood would be all over the place, instead of just around her neck. Be more of it too."

Schwartz shook his head sadly. "Had to be sure, I guess. However... How long's she been dead?"

"About an hour, roughly."

"All right. Now, Nelson, how'd you happen to come here and find her?"

"Miss Patterson was in the company of a man I wanted to

At Millicent's "hello," Harvey almost
dropped off the chair. She was with Bonzetti!
Pembroke was smiling sardonically

talk to," Harvey explained. "Having been told that he might be here, I asked the room clerk downstairs. He told me that Miss Patterson had left him at the elevator in the lobby and that he had then left the place. I thought she might know where he had gone, so I came up to ask her."

"He left the place, eh? Who was he?"

"Daniel Danvers," said Harvey.

"The politician, eh? Now what else do you know about this Dolly Patterson? Her friends and otherwise."

"Can't help you," said Harvey. "An hour ago I didn't even know her name. I only learned it when I inquired where Danvers might be. Is there anything else? Miss Forbes is suffering from shock. I'd like to take her home."

Schwartz scratched his chin and pondered for a minute. "No," he finally said. "Thanks a lot for your help. But keep yourself available in case I need you."

"Omega! Stay here and work on this man Schwartz! Don't go!"
"Gotta go. I can't leave Harvey till I get more strength. It took all I had to get back. Stay with me, or you'll find yourself back at the creek!"

MILLICENT WAS silent all the way down the elevator and through the lobby. She didn't open her mouth until the door of a cab slammed shut on them, and he absently took the coveted lists from his pocket. Neither of them noticed that a second cab pulled away from the curb directly behind theirs.

"Harvey Nelson!" she said. "I don't know what to make of you."

Harvey looked up from his perusal of the papers. "What's the matter?" he asked, slightly confused. "She didn't mind."

Millicent sighed in exasperation. "I don't mean her. She wouldn't have minded anyway, I was referring to your underhand trick back in that room. Oh, don't look so innocent. You know you mentioned Danvers' name on purpose. Was that fair?"

Harvey chuckled. "Can't withhold information from the police," he told her. "How do I know but what he might provide the lead which will catch the murderer? Besides, I had to explain why we were there. I couldn't mention these lists."

Millicent slumped back in her seat. "I still don't know what to make of you," she said, wearily. "For the past two days you've been a different man entirely."

"Listen, sweetheart," Harvey pleaded. "Things are happening fast, and I've been inattentive because my mind is in a whirl. When we get everything straightened out I'll make it up to you. Right now all I can think of is to get Fowler elected and clean house in this town."

"Sort of a military objective, eh? You're so single-minded about it that you'll even withhold information which might bring a murderer to justice." *Sniff!*

"Milly!" he said, reproachfully. "I couldn't tell Schwartz about these papers. All I know myself is what Omega told me. And he learned it by reading Danvers' and Dolly's minds. If I told him what I know, he wouldn't believe me. And unless he knew the whole story those lists would just cause a lot of trouble without doing any good. But I can put them to excellent purpose."

Millicent didn't seem to be listening. She hunched over in her seat and smiled up at him coyly.

"I love you just the same," she confided. Then she hesitated before she whispered: "Is Omega still asleep?"

Harvey gathered her in his arms and kissed her tenderly. "I almost forgot him," he said. "Do you know this is the first time we've been really alone since he arrived? We ought to do something about it…"

Millicent snuggled closer, but said nothing.

"Yes," repeated Harvey. "We should do something about it. We can't have him plaguing us all our lives. Didn't you say you had an idea on the subject?"

Millicent stared directly in front for a long minute. Then: "He's a shadow," said Millicent. "And no matter how dark it is there's always enough light for him. But suppose there were light, blinding light, on all sides of you? Where would he be then?"

Harvey pondered. "Gone, I guess," he answered. "But he's been gone several times. And he always comes back."

"So you told me. But on those times he's only been asleep. My idea is that if he were suddenly subjected to intense light from all directions, while he's in full possession of his faculties, maybe he would be shocked back to normal. He might become a decent respectable shadow, the way he was before he came to life."

Harvey didn't answer for a while. When he did his voice was very sober.

"I don't think I could bring myself to do it," he said. "If he didn't show up again I'd always think of myself as a murderer. He *is* alive, you know."

CHAPTER XVI

COME NOW, MR. BONZETTI!

THE CAB PULLED up in front of Millicent's apartment house, and Harvey was silent as they rode up in the elevator. Millicent, apparently sad about the turn of affairs, was lost in her thoughts. Neither saw the trouble the elevator boy was experiencing with his controls, but they were jarred back to the present when the cage slammed against the top of the shaft.

"Darn it, Mr. Nelson," complained the operator. "You'll get me in trouble doing that. Don't you know it's after midnight? I'm liable to lose—"

He turned his head as he talked, and suddenly gasped. For Harvey was on the other side of the elevator. Millicent was between him and the controls.

"Oh I'm sorry, Mr. Nelson," the boy hastened to apologize. "I could have sworn… It must be this lever. It won't move!"

The boy wrenched at the lever, and suddenly it swung back and dropped the car. Harvey handed the boy a bill and told him to refer his boss to him, if anything was said about the noise. He'd vouch for the fact that the lever had jammed.

"Just wanted you to know that I was around all the time," whispered Omega. "I heard what you said."

He didn't make any other comment, and Harvey was suddenly too weary to answer. He kissed Millicent goodnight and promised her that as soon as he cleared up the matter of the election, he'd put his colossal intellect to work on the other problem.

She went into her apartment looking a bit happier. A whole lot happier, in fact, than Harvey felt.

He went down in the elevator, while the operator watched him furtively—and somewhat suspiciously. Harvey didn't notice him. He was still deep in thought as he climbed into a taxi at the curb. Too engrossed, by far, to notice that a second cab again followed immediately after.

"What are you going to do?" came the voice in Harvey's brain.

"Go back to Patelli's," growled Harvey, half aloud.

"I don't mean that," said Omega. "I mean about me. Are you going to try the light trick?"

"Will it work?" countered Harvey.

There was a long silence. Then, "I don't know. It might."

"Why did you ask?" Harvey suddenly inquired. "I thought you could read my mind."

"So I can, to a certain extent. But lately I find it's getting harder. You've built up a resistance against my probing. It's easier to ask, now."

PATELLI WAS in his private office when Harvey arrived. Spread on a desk before him were several notebooks, varying in size from small memo books to one large ledger.

"I hope these will help," he said. "But listen: this stuff is dynamite, so don't let it get out of your hands. Take what pages you want and give me back the rest."

Harvey blinked rapidly at some of the names entered in the books. But he resolutely passed over the portions which didn't apply to the party donations. These men were trusting him not to see too much, and it wouldn't help a bit to double-cross them.

Some of the names he noticed, and the items recorded beside them, would have raised hob if ever made public. Harvey wasn't interested. He had an objective, and he was sticking to it. He took a sharp penknife from his pocket and cut out a page which dealt with party donations over a period of several months.

In another ledger he found relevant items, and removed a

page by snapping clips in the binding. One other book had loose-leaf pages, and he removed three from it. The rest required the penknife.

When he was finished there were ten pages in a pile, all dealing with payments made to the party fund, by men who had wished to continue their illegitimate vocations. In each case the payments had increased in amount, from month to month, as Pembroke had become greedier and greedier.

The top sums, when the payments ceased, represented the point known as All the Traffic Will Bear. The next increase, Harvey deduced, was the one which had put the man out of business. Pembroke had become too greedy. He hadn't known where to stop.

"These, coupled with some other stuff, will lick Pembroke," he told Patelli. "Give my thanks to the men who handed them over. I'll return them some time tomorrow." He glanced at his wrist watch. "Today, I mean."

A man who had been listening outside the door barely dodged back in the shadows as Harvey came out, tucking a long envelope in his inside pocket. The man followed at a discreet distance as Harvey left the club, once more entering a taxi. He dashed for the next one in line and ordered the driver to follow.

There was a mystified expression on the man's wind-burned face, and also a trace of determination. Even the fact that his supply of ready cash was being woefully depleted with all this cab riding failed to lessen this doggedness. He resolved that if the man in the cab ahead went too far with such extravagance, he would keep on his trail by hopping on the bumper when he started off.

The first cab stopped in the middle of a block. He hastily ordered his own driver to stop some distance behind. He fished in a pocket and brought forth a notebook. He rapidly thumbed through it until he came to the right page.

"Hell," he grunted, half aloud. "That's where he lives. I better get some sleep myself. And some dough, too."

A few minutes later he was carefully setting an alarm clock for seven o'clock, four hours hence. Thence he laid his clothes where he could jump into them in a hurry, and went to sleep.

HARVEY OPENED the street door to his quarters, and fixed the latch so the door could be opened without a key. Then he sprinted up the flight of stairs and did likewise with the door at the top.

A second later he was at the window, peering up the street. He was rewarded by the sight of a taxi driving off. He smiled grimly and seated himself in an easy chair beside a small writing desk. Still in the dark he opened a drawer and removed an efficient army automatic.

Harvey hadn't missed seeing the man who had dodged aside when he left Patelli's. He had also seen him trail his cab. And now, Harvey decided, the man was on his way back to report to Bonzetti that his victim was safely in his flat.

Harvey smiled again, and patted the gun in his hand. He didn't intend to take a chance on letting himself be kidnapped now. With enough evidence to force a confession out of Danvers, there was no need for it.

He settled back further in the chair and waited. His eyes tried to droop, but he forced them to stay open. It wouldn't do to have Bonzetti barge in and find him asleep.

The only trouble with trying to stay awake in the dark was the fact that his eyelids could close and he wouldn't know it. He lit a cigarette. It scorched his finger a minute later, and he put it out. He wondered vaguely if a man could fall asleep with his eyes open. It was dark anyway. Did eyelids have to be closed in order to sleep?

"Can't you get away yet?"

"No. Tried a couple times. Too weak. You're to blame for this! Suppose I have to live through this man's whole lifetime, stuck here in the past?"

"You're really his shadow now, eh? Haven't you strength enough to send me to watch Schwartz? That might help."

"No. It's all I can do to keep you here. Maybe if I let you drift back to your own time, I'd have strength enough to release myself from Harvey, though. I'll try that if I can't get loose."

"Don't do that! Harvey's about to be kidnapped! Stay with him and help out. He's in real trouble. And you're to blame for that. Don't forget it."

"How in the name of—All right. I'm to blame for it. But that don't say I'm going to stay here the rest of his life and watch over him. He's big enough…"

CHAPTER XVII

MILLY'S CHILLY

MILLICENT FORBES WAS a nice girl. She had put up a pretense of being happy and contented with Harvey's promise to put his mind down to the problem of Omega. That was only because she was a nice girl and didn't want to worry him. He had enough worries.

But as a matter of fact Millicent wasn't happy at all. She was miserable—as Harvey could have easily seen if he hadn't been on the opposite side of her door when she closed it. For Millicent slumped wearily in a chair and gazed blankly at the wall. Tears welled up in her eyes and she angrily blinked them out. Unheeded then, they furrowed a way through her lightly-applied makeup.

She listened to the clang of the elevator doors and went into the bedroom. She spent some time undressing, washing and applying creams, but the ritual failed to cheer her as it usually did.

Harvey's promise, for the first time since she could remember, wasn't much good. The very fact that he postponed the solution to that problem revealed that he hadn't the slightest hope that anything could be done about it. Procrastination wasn't one of his faults. When Harvey had a problem, he went after it immediately.

The thing was fantastic anyway. Shadows were impalpable things, not given to talking back. Where you went, they went,

and never argued about it. But something had happened, something completely outside the realm of human understanding.

For Harvey's shadow was really alive, and decidedly frisky.
She couldn't ignore it—or him, as this shadow must properly be
designated. As a husband Harvey would be impossible—unless
something were done.

Millicent climbed into bed and pulled up the covers. The
pillow felt cool; then after a minute, slightly damp. Annoyed,
she wiped her eyes and turned it over. Sternly she forced her
mind into other channels, determined to forget all about it and
go to sleep.

That, of course, was a mistake. Sleep can't be bullied. And
besides, her mind refused to co-operate. It returned to Harvey
of its own volition.

For three years she had loved him, sometimes almost hope-
lessly. She had admired his kindness and the idealistic view he
took of everything around him. Lately he had changed, losing
some of his trustfulness and replacing it with a better insight
into the motives of those he associated with.

But his ideals were still there. Intensified, if anything. She
loved him more for the change; for it had enabled him to get
up the nerve to propose. He had lost some of his shyness, the
thing which had kept him from the step before.

Millicent half believed that Omega had something to do with
it all, though she couldn't be sure. If he had, then she owed him a
debt. And that thought brought her back to her main problem.
Harvey had said that he had come to regard his encumbrance as
another human, an entity which couldn't be eliminated without
destroying a life. He had even come to develop a certain fond-
ness for him.

And now that she thought it over, Millicent wasn't so sure
that it *wouldn't* be murder ruthlessly to destroy Omega—provid-
ing, of course, that it could he done at all. He was a likable cuss
at that.

Sleep finally came, though it was fitful at first and broken by dreams of Omega interfering all through the years to come. When she woke there was still the feeling of futility and sorrow which had gripped her when she had said goodnight to Harvey. For several seconds she lay in bed, staring at nothing, trying to get her thoughts in order. Until a gentle rap sounded at the door.

Hastily donning a housecoat, she answered, opening the door a few inches. A heavy man in a business suit smiled at her. He flipped open the lapel of his coat and Millicent caught a fleeting look at a shield.

"Headquarters," said the man. "Lieutenant Schwartz would like to have you sign a statement. Mr. Nelson is over there now. I've got a car downstairs if you'd like to come right away."

"I'll be ready in a jiffy," she said, opening the door wider. "Make yourself comfortable while I dress. There's liquor in the cabinet."

The man's eyes widened as he accepted the invitation. "Lady," he said as she disappeared into the bedroom, "you're a gentleman."

He managed to slug down four drinks out of a brown bottle, and was eyeing a green bottle distrustfully and trying to decipher certain words in Italian on the label, when she reappeared, fully dressed.

At first Millicent didn't notice that the car was already occupied. The man who sat in the back seat was in shadow and wore a dark suit. It was too late to jump out when she did see him, for he had a pistol pointed at her. She did hesitate, but he reached out the other hand and pulled her the rest of the way inside. The door slammed behind her.

"I always have to supervise these things myself," he said, conversationally. "That's why Lucky Bonzetti stays out of jail. Get goin', Barney."

MILLICENT SIGHED and relaxed in the seat. She clucked sympathetically. "It is a bore, isn't it? Not being able to depend on your hired help."

Bonzetti nodded. "Yeah," he agreed. "Understand, they're

dependable. They won't cross me up, or anything. But they're dumb. They ain't smart, like Lucky Bonzetti. They make mistakes, and that's bad in my business."

"Where are we going?" asked Millicent.

"A nice place, toots. You'll like it, though you'll only be there for a few weeks."

"Only a few weeks?"

"Sure, sure, just till after the primaries."

Millicent nodded calmly, as if the matter were quite the usual thing. "I thought it was something like that," she said.

"Say, you're pretty cool, ain't you." Bonzetti observed. "That's the way I like 'em. Saves a lot of trouble."

"Oh, I wouldn't want to be any trouble," said Millicent. "I know it's all a matter of business. Nothing personal."

Bonzetti nodded and looked at her admiringly. "That's the proper attitude. I wish more people realized that, instead of getting all excited and raising a fuss."

Millicent idly watched the city flow past the car window and noted that they were approaching the edge of town. She could see through the glass of the door, obliquely, but well enough to recognize the route. There weren't any windows at the sides of the back seat, and the curtain was pulled down over the rear window.

To a person outside the car both she and Bonzetti were probably invisible in the shadows. Bonzetti at least made no attempt to conceal his gun. She noticed that he kept it pointed in her general direction, in spite of her docile manner. She had hoped that he would relax, but the scheme didn't work. Bonzetti was smart.

The car reached the edge of the city and continued, picking up speed. Then it slowed suddenly and turned into a side road. After a short distance it stopped under a tree.

"I guess you won't object to a blindfold," Bonzetti ventured. "Part of the business, you know."

"Not at all," said Millicent, agreeably. "Be careful with my hair, though. It's a new wave."

The gangster covered her eyes effectively with a black silk handkerchief, carefully tying it in the back under her curls. "You're pretty good, you are," he declared. "How'd you ever come to hook up with a guy like Harvey Nelson?"

"Oh, he has his points," said Millicent. "Though at times, he is hard to get along with. He's always banging his head against a stone wall. Like trying to make politicians give the public a break. It can't be done."

"You said it," agreed Bonzetti. "But I figure he ought to have had more sense than to buck Pembroke. That guy'd double-cross his own mother."

MILLICENT WAS silent for a moment, thinking about the excuse which had brought her out of her apartment. No doubt Bonzetti had read about the murder in the morning papers and decided it would make a good story to get her to come peaceably. And then again…

"That business in Dolly Patterson's apartment," she began. "Was that one of your jobs? I thought it was pretty neat. There didn't seem to be a clue, except that the place had been searched thoroughly."

Bonzetti's eyes narrowed. Millicent couldn't see that, of course, but she sensed that the man beside her had tensed a bit. There was a pause before he answered, and when he did there was a different tone to his voice. It was slightly colder, less affable and friendly.

"Thoroughly, eh? Then you figure the one who searched it found what he was looking for?"

Millicent didn't answer right away. Not because she didn't know what to say, but because she was trying to keep her mind straight on the number of turns the car had made since she had been blindfolded. She gave it up, though, for she suddenly realized that some of them had been natural turns of a winding country road, and that she couldn't be sure which ones were actual changes to another road. It didn't matter anyway. Knowing where she was wouldn't help her escape.

"I don't know," she answered. "He might have found it in the last place he looked. Then again he mightn't have."

"I get it," said Bonzetti, suddenly thawing. "If the place had only been half searched, you could be sure the guy found it. Or maybe was scared before he finished. So it looks to me like he didn't find it. And I bet I know the answer!"

"What?"

"Your boy friend found the papers! Right?"

"Papers? What papers?"

Bonzetti laughed, apparently very pleased. "Never mind," he chuckled. "I got it all now. This Dolly had swiped some papers off Danvers. Why, I don't know. But it's a good chance that they were bad business for Pembroke. Because he asked me to put the dame on the spot and get them back. But my price being too high, he said he'd get somebody else. And that somebody else botched the job!" Bonzetti finished with another roar of laughter.

There was comparative silence for a few minutes, broken only by the whine of tires which had moved onto a stretch of concrete or some other smooth surface, and by the occasional chuckle of Bonzetti. He was probably having a lot of fun thinking about the results of Pembroke's hiring a less able agent to do his dirty work. Millicent began to get fidgety.

"Where are we going?" she asked again.

"A nice place, like I said," Bonzetti insisted. "Say, I was just thinking; we're going to be cooped up for quite a while."

Millicent groaned inwardly. "And you've got ideas, of course," she observed.

"Why not? I've sorta taken a shine to you. You seem to be a pretty sensible fem, and—"

THE CAR gave a sudden jolt as it turned abruptly up a rough country lane. Bonzetti grabbed a strap at his side and placed his gun in its holster. For a couple of minutes it was necessary for both of them to keep their jaws tightly clenched to prevent biting off their tongues. Then came a surging stop which almost threw them from the seat.

"Here we are, boss," came Barney's cheerful voice. "That road needs a going over."

"*You* need a going over," rasped Bonzetti. "If you ever give me a ride like that again, I'll make you drink a gallon of nitro and then I'll push you off City Hall!"

"I hate to slow down, boss," Barney said, lamely. "Sorry if I—"

Bonzetti made a vicious pass, but allowed it to fall just short of Barney's jaw. This was another evidence of his braininess; for if Barney had actually been struck, his slow moving brain might not have worked in time to prevent him from hitting back. And that would have been bad for morale, especially if he had flattened his boss. And that probably is what would have happened, Barney being about fifty pounds heavier.

Bonzetti's rage evaporated as he looked at Millicent. His face softened and then looked regretful. Still being careful of her curls, he untied the blindfold. She blinked at the sudden light and then smiled.

"I'm outa the mood now," he stated. "I'll talk to you later. Besides, I got an important phone call to make."

Bonzetti turned and entered a stone bungalow which set back from the driveway. A large calloused hand took Millicent's elbow.

"Don't mind him, sister," said Barney. "He always has them moods. Now me, I'm different. I'm always in the mood, come to think of it. So don't go pining away…"

"I wasn't pining away," Millicent assured him. "I was merely looking at the house. It does seem to be a nice place. Shall we go in?"

Bonzetti had put through his telephone call. He turned and beckoned as she entered the living room. "It's your boy friend," he said, chuckling. "Tell him I'm going to take good care of you."

CHAPTER XVIII

THE LIFE OF O'REILLY

HARVEY WOKE UP with a splitting headache, and vaguely wondered why. Then he suddenly remembered. He jumped to his feet and looked at his watch. Eight o'clock. He hadn't been kidnapped after all! He might just as well have gone to bed. A dozen aches in a dozen muscles amplified the thought.

Hastily he stripped off his rumpled clothes and headed for the bathroom. He winced as stabs of pain shot through his head, but there wasn't much he could do about it. A cup of coffee, when he got time for it, would fix the headache. In the meantime...

He fumbled in a medicine closet for a moment and pulled out a bottle filled with a brownish liquid. There was a skull and crossed bones on the label, but that didn't deter him in the least. He tilted it, pouring every last drop down his throat.

"What's the skull for?" Omega asked.

Harvey started, guiltily. "I'd forgotten you," he said, a bit, unsteadily. "That's to indicate poison, so nobody will drink it by mistake."

"You drank it," Omega pointed out.

"Not by mistake," Harvey said, dashing cold water on his face. "I drank it on purpose."

"Then it's not poison, except by mistake, eh?"

Harvey dried himself briskly. "I've got friends," he explained, laboriously. "They drink everything in sight sometimes. But they won't drink poison. Therefore I always have an eye-opener left when I wake up. I'll refill that, first chance I get, with the finest poison on the market."

Harvey was changing clothes as he talked, and occasionally casting a glance at the clock. He finished hurriedly, and headed for the door.

"Wait a minute," came Omega's wail. "I want my duds, too."

Harvey groaned. "Not this time, please," he said. "I've got to get a confession out of Danvers and I haven't much time. Please!"

There was a silence during which Harvey quaked inwardly and involuntarily braced himself against a punch in the stomach. Finally Omega said, "All right. I don't want to cause any trouble." He sounded so dejected that Harvey almost told him to get dressed, but he caught himself in time and strode out the door.

He didn't call a taxi, but instead headed for a repair shop a block away. His car was in running order, the bumper straightened and the blown tire replaced. He drove off feeling much better. His headache was tapering off; a cup of coffee would ease it completely if he could find time for one. The morning air and the urgency of the work to be done had sharpened his mind and made him forget his other problems.

If he could have seen the grim though slightly bewildered face in the following cab, he mightn't have felt so chipper.

THE MAN in the cab didn't feel so chipper himself. His four hours of sleep, instead of the usual nine or ten, made him somewhat gloomy. He was beginning to wonder if he wasn't on a wild goose chase.

Not that his determination had faltered; not in the least. He was going to see this thing through. But up to the present he couldn't see where he was doing much good. Maybe he should have called in some wiser heads on this quest. Maybe he didn't have the brain for this kind of work.

He tried to piece together some sense from the things he had learned. Somehow they didn't seem to add up. He'd seen Nelson take his girl home. That didn't mean anything. He'd seen him get some papers from Patelli, night club operator and former gambler. That meant something, all right, but he hadn't the slightest idea what. If he only knew what those papers were...

The car ahead finally stopped at a pretentious place, set back from the road, almost at the edge of town. The wind-burnt man left the cab and followed. He saw a chance to approach the house unobserved, by taking advantage of the copious shrubbery which surrounded it. He peeked in the windows from time to time, and was finally rewarded by the sight of Nelson entering the library, followed by a middle-aged, prosperous-looking man with a worried look on his dignified face.

The man at the window jumped involuntarily. He knew that face; it belonged to Dan Danvers, party treasurer and a man who had been mentioned as possible mayor. Danvers looked decidedly worried as he slumped in an armchair. Nelson stood over him and banged his fist on a table as if he were threatening him.

The man wished he could hear what was going on. It would have solved the mystery, he was sure.

Pembroke laid it on the line to Harvey: "I get what I want, and that's all that matters."

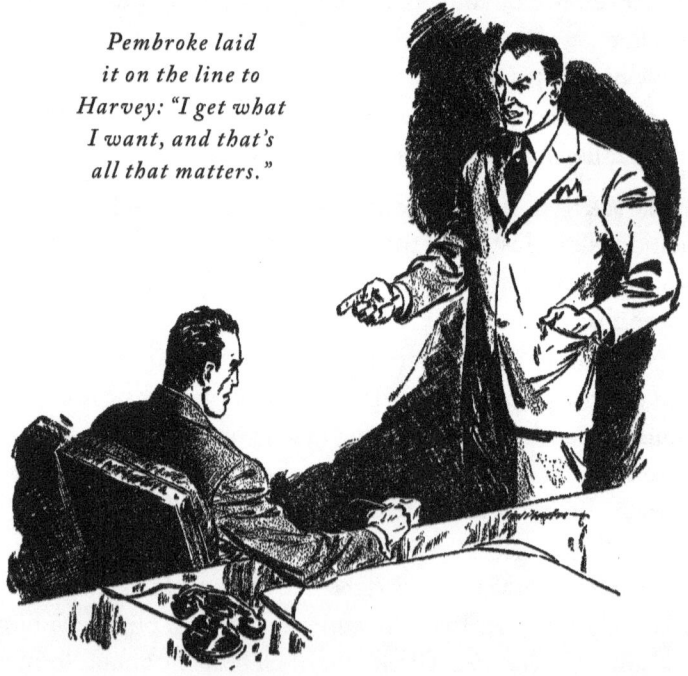

Nelson seemed to be talking volumes, and getting red in the face as he talked. Danvers slumped further in the chair as he listened. Finally he got up and crossed the room to a desk, which he opened.

The angle was bad but the man at the window interpreted what he saw to mean that Danvers was writing something, and that Nelson was dictating it. He could only see Danvers' back from this angle, but it was hunched over as when a man is writing.

Finally Danvers straightened; Nelson leaned over and picked up a paper. He was smiling triumphantly as he did this, and the wind-burnt man thought it high time to get back to his cab.

Harvey was still smiling when he returned to his car. He didn't notice as he drove off towards Pembroke's offices that a cab was doing its very best to keep up with him. Harvey was driving at quite a clip, and the cab had been built more for endurance than for speed.

"I don't blame Milly for saying you've changed," remarked Omega. "You used to drive like a snail with arthritis."

"There's work to be done," chortled Harvey. "How did you like the way I handled Danvers?"

"Couldn't have done better myself," Omega admitted. "You're a changed man. A week ago he could have denied the whole thing—called it an optical illusion—and you'd have believed him."

"Hardly that bad," said Harvey, pulling up in front of the Bugle building. "Though I'll admit I was a little scared for a minute or two that he wouldn't bluff."

There was a slight altercation behind Harvey as he started into the building. A cab had pulled up and let out a passenger who didn't like the size of his bill and wasn't hesitating about saying so. But Harvey had other things on his mind and didn't turn. He continued toward the bank of elevators.

"Mr. Nelson! Mr. Nelson!" came an urgent voice behind him.

"Hello, O'Reilly," said Harvey. "Where are you going?"

"With you." O'Reilly said it defiantly, as if challenging any possible denial of his right to do so.

HARVEY LOOKED puzzled, but nodded; headed for the building's lunch room. He sat down on a stool and ordered coffee, black. He nodded again, absently, as O'Reilly lifted two fingers to the waiter behind the counter. But when the waiter delivered the two cups, he snapped out of his reverie and suddenly asked, "Why?"

O'Reilly was confused for a second, as his face plainly revealed, but rallied determinedly.

"I'm working on that Dolly Patterson murder, on my own," he said. "And I'm staying with you till I find out something. I'm gonna get the jump on that guy Schwartz if I have to tie myself to you."

Harvey looked at him wonderingly. "I don't get it," he said.

O'Reilly dropped two lumps in his coffee before replying. "I figure you do," he finally said. "I saw something in that room that maybe the others didn't. There was a little crescent-shaped line of blood on the carpet, about a foot away from the puddle under the girl's head. Then there was a very faint line, same shape and same size, about five feet nearer to where you were standing when we came in.

"I figure that you accidentally touched the puddle with the tip of your toe. Your girl's shoes were pointed, so it had to be yours. The first mark was made when you shifted your weight, and the second was made when you stepped away. A guy your size takes about two and a half feet to a step."

Harvey nodded and glanced briefly at the toes of his shoes. "The thick carpet wiped it off," he said. "But what makes you think I know something about the murder? It's perfectly natural that I would step over and make sure that the girl was dead and beyond any help."

"That's what I thought at first," O'Reilly confessed. "But then I happened to think that anybody could see a mile away that she had to be dead. With a gash like that, and a bucket of blood…"

Harvey refused to comment, merely maintaining a noncommittal expression as he waited for the state trooper to continue.

"… So I got to figuring that a man's left foot would come pretty close to that puddle if he stooped down to search the body. The medical examiner's did. It just struck me then, that if you had been telling a phoney story to Schwartz, maybe your real reason for going there was to get the same thing that the murderer had been searching for. And that maybe you looked for it on the body. That would mean that you knew what the guy was searching for, and therefore why she was killed. You get the idea?"

Harvey nodded. "An awful lot of maybes," he observed.

"I though it was a good piece of deductive reasoning," said O'Reilly, expanding slightly.

"Well, I don't know a thing about it," said Harvey, flatly.

"What! But you admitted." O'Reilly was aghast. His face went pale, then flooded with color. Such surprises play havoc with a man's blood pressure.

"I ADMITTED nothing except that I may have stepped in the puddle of blood," said Harvey. "If I was lying to Schwartz, and if I stooped over to search the body, then the rest is true. That only trouble is I wasn't lying. I told Schwartz that an hour before the thing happened. I didn't even know the lady's name. I also told him that I was after Danvers, only going to her apartment because I had been told he was with her. And that's the truth."

O'Reilly shoved his hat back on his head and scratched. He did it in a way which suggested that he really didn't expect to find anything, or relieve any particular itch, but rather as a gesture intended to stimulate the gray matter which he assumed to be under his moving fingers.

"I guess I don't have the head for this work," he admitted. "I could have sworn there was something… Oh, I remember. What were the papers you got from Patelli?"

Harvey started in surprise. "You've been following me ever

since then?" he asked. "Then you were the man who drove off in a cab after I went into my flat last night."

"Yeah," O'Reilly grinned. "I went home to get a little sleep."

Harvey grinned, too. "Those papers were private business," he said. "Something which can be explained, if necessary, as plausibly as the matter of my presence in that room."

That O'Reilly didn't like his answer was immediately discernible. Harvey could almost see his mind trying to figure out the next move and so Harvey chose that particular moment to make a quick dash for the elevators. One was opening as he started and he made it with plenty to spare.

O'Reilly tried, but Harvey's sprint had been too sudden for him. The elevator starter clicked his little cricket and the doors slammed shut before he got near them. He fumed and waited for the next car, meanwhile eyeing the arrow which showed the floor stops of the elevator he had missed. Then he turned morosely away and leaned against a wall. The darned thing had stopped three times while he had watched it.

CHAPTER XIX

TWO WEEKS TO DEATH

PEMBROKE, LOOKING QUITE happy, greeted his visitor with a smile and an extended hand.

"Nelson," he said, before Harvey could open his mouth, "the time has about come for you and me to get together. You've been pretty smart in the past, and I think I can make you see things my way. In fact I was just going to send for you. We have some talking to do."

Harvey smiled amiably. "We certainly have," he said, taking Danvers' confession and placing it on Pembroke's desk. "Look this over before we talk."

Pembroke's poker face revealed nothing as he read the paper carefully and then looked at the ceiling for a long minute. Finally he finished his inspection and evidently concluded that the thing was in no immediate danger of falling, for he lowered his eyes and appraised Harvey carefully.

"You're a smart lad," he observed. "Those lists you got from Dolly Patterson wouldn't have been of much use, except as a means of getting this confession. And the other stuff wouldn't have been of any use at all if Danvers hadn't confessed that he turned all money from such sources over to me. Very clever. However, it was all very unnecessary."

Harvey's eyes narrowed. "What do you mean?"

"It's the same every time," Pembroke said, reflectively. "Someone thinks he can outsmart the old master, and then gets mad when he finds it can't be done. Take a seat, Nelson. I'm waiting for a phone call." He glanced at a clock on the opposite side of the room. "It should have come a couple of minutes ago."

It came. A muted jangling arose from a point beneath the desk. Pembroke reached for the phone. "Wonderful timing," he observed, lifting it from the cradle. After his barked, "Pembroke!" he listened for a moment and remarked. "Okay, I'm putting Nelson on," and handed the instrument to Harvey.

At Millicent's "Hello," Harvey almost dropped the phone. He looked at Pembroke, who was smiling sardonically. Harvey realized that he was licked, thoroughly. Pembroke had talked to Bonzetti after all, but he had arranged to kidnap Milly, not him.

Harvey swallowed, to regain control of paralyzed vocal chords.

"Where are you?" he whispered hoarsely.

"Don't know," said Millicent, her voice shaking in spite of an effort to control it. "Bonzetti blindfolded me."

"Listen carefully," Harvey said, after a pause. "They're going to demand that I support Danvers in return for your continued health. And I'm going to do it—just so long as I hear your voice over the phone whenever I demand it. Now put Bonzetti on and I'll straighten things out."

Harvey turned to Pembroke, who had been listening interestedly. "You're going to give Bonzetti orders to keep his hands off her," he said. "I'll support Danvers as long as she's treated right. The instant she's molested I'm going to blow the works. I'm holding these papers until I get her back."

Pembroke hesitated, thoughtfully. Then, he shrugged his shoulders and picked up the telephone. Briefly and forcefully he told Bonzetti what Harvey demanded. Then he hung up and smiled.

"It's a good arrangement," he said. "I get what I want and that's all that matters. Bonzetti holds your girl until the election is over. As soon as Danvers gets the nomination you and I make our trade. Millicent Forbes in return for those lists, and Danvers' confession. Agreed?"

HARVEY LEFT, his mind seething. Pembroke, the master strategist; knew when he had gained his immediate objective. But there was one weak link in the arrangement; and if Pembroke hadn't thought of it yet, he certainly would later. For as long as Millicent was alive and free, she was a danger to Bonzetti; and he in turn was a danger to Pembroke.

The obvious answer was that neither Bonzetti nor Pembroke could afford to turn her loose. And, also obviously, Harvey was bound by his agreement to exactly the extent to which Pembroke was bound. Which was not at all.

Temporarily at least, Millicent was safe. Election day was two weeks away and Millicent would be treated all right as long as his efforts were necessary to nominate Danvers. But after that—what then? Harvey growled audibly as the elevator door slammed shut. There was only one answer and that was to start work immediately to find her. By election day Millicent must be free; or the day after she would be dead.

> *"Did you read Pembroke's mind?" Mark demanded. "Where's Milly?"*
>
> *"Couldn't. I'm too weak yet. Even thought impulses don't register unless they're sent with an effort, as yours are. I can't seem—I think maybe I'd better send you back to the present. Then I'd be able to recuperate my strength. I'm getting worried."*
>
> *"No! I have no way of knowing what's happened while I'm gone. Hold on to me."*
>
> *"Don't be silly! This all happened six thousand years ago."*
>
> *"But you're changing it. It's happening differently now."*
>
> *"I wonder."*

The elevator stopped at the lobby floor. Harvey growled again. O'Reilly grinned like a playful puppy and fell into step.

"What were you doing upstairs?" he asked, as if he really expected an answer.

"I don't like the men's washrooms on the ground floor," answered Harvey, increasing the length of his stride until O'Reilly fell slightly to the rear.

This wasn't because the state cop was short, for he was fully as tall as Harvey, but rather because his legs weren't quite as long. Harvey opened the door of his car and sat down. O'Reilly sprinted to the other side, intent upon stealing a free ride. But he met an outstretched arm as he attempted to open the door.

On the end of this arm was an open hand, something really phenomenal in hands, one which had stopped many a skillful tackler. It stopped O'Reilly, snapped his head back so suddenly that the bones of his neck crunched together in an alarming manner. By the time he had straightened the neck and determined that it would still support his head with some degree of stability, Harvey's car had roared out from beneath his outraged nose.

Officer O'Reilly really suffered as he saw the pleased expression on the face of the cab driver when he demanded that he follow the speeding sedan. It seemed that the fellow actually knew that he was getting a chance to get even with constabulary in general.

Harvey drove furiously, while his mind did its best to keep, pace. This was a bad combination of activities, for he was thinking of other things besides driving. The result was a series of close ones; but finally he arrived at his destination in one piece. Physically at least. Patelli's club was the destination.

A hostile-eyed bartender took his order for a double scotch, straight. Harvey had never seen the man before, no doubt because his working hours didn't extend into the evening.

"Where's Patelli?" asked Harvey.

"Home in bed, I guess," said the man. "What d'ya want?"

"Where's he live?"

The bartender gestured.

"He's in the phone book, if you really want to know. You don't catch me sending a salesman around to wake him up."

Harvey slugged down the drink, muttered under his breath, and found a directory. Sure enough, Patelli was listed. Harvey wasted no time in calling him. He watched the door to the club as he listened to the buzz of the bell ringer. He half expected to see O'Reilly pop in, wild-eyed.

Something else popped, however.

A sudden roar sounded in his ear. He moved the receiver an inch or so away, and gradually the sound became articulate, though sulphurous. He understood why the bartender wanted no part in the waking of Patelli. It was a job for a lion tamer.

"Take it easy, Joe," he soothed. "This is Harvey Nelson. Something's come up that's more important than anybody's sleep. I've got to talk to you, right away. Shall I come up, or will you see me at the club?"

There was a short pause. Then: "Come up here. It'll be quicker."

Harvey noted the address, at the northern end of town, and sprinted for the curb. His car roared down the one-way street and made a forbidden left turn at Broad, a through street north and south. Several whistles blew before he reached Patelli's address, but Harvey didn't slow down in the least. He'd collect a flock of summonses, of course, but he'd take care of them later.

Right now he had to get the machinery started, and the machinery he was thinking of might turn out to be almost as ponderous as that of the law which he couldn't enlist. Two weeks could, upon occasion, go past with startling speed.

By election day Milly must be free; or the day after *she'd be dead.*

CHAPTER XX

O'REILLY EATS FREE

PATELLI'S PLACE WAS in a restricted neighborhood in the best section of the city. The architecture was a bit lurid, but then Mr. Patelli was slightly lurid himself. His tastes were tended to run to the picturesque, more often than not. Harvey was greeted by a butler who would have looked about right either at the door of a club or at the bridge of a naval flagship.

"Come right in, sir," he said. "The master is waiting for you. I'll take care of your skimmer."

Harvey handed the man his hat and followed him into a library. He strode back and forth, too agitated to take the indicated chair, and that was probably the reason for the butler's puzzled head-shake as he left the room. Harvey guessed that this particular butler had obtained his experience from a book, and was consequently annoyed when people didn't act according to the rules. He'd probably been a bouncer in Patelli's gambling joint before his boss had gone legitimate.

Patelli bounced into the room, struggling with a smoking jacket. "What's up?" he wanted to know.

Harvey told him, sparing no detail. "And now," he finished, "the problem is to locate her. That's why I've come to you. Where would Bonzetti hide her?"

Patelli looked worried. "That guy's bad business," he said. "I'd hate to—"

"But you've got to help me!" Harvey insisted. "If we let Pembroke get away with this, he'll rule the town with an iron hand. He'll use this administration to make a final clean-up, knowing full well that each succeeding election has been getting harder to swing. He'll have his cut out of every club in town, until he takes all the profit out of it. And besides, think of Milly."

"That's who I'm thinking of," said Patelli, quietly. "I ain't worrying about Danvers getting in."

Harvey fell suddenly silent. He realized that he had misjudged Patelli; and he wanted to get his thoughts in order. The stubby club owner was human; he had forgotten that for the moment. He had been regarding Patelli as a man who would appreciate nothing less than an appeal to his pocketbook.

"I'll have to round up the boys," Patelli continued. "Between us we might be able to get a lead. Don't get up too much hope, though. You go back to the club and wait. I'll call as soon as I learn anything."

Harvey thanked him and left, assured that inside an hour there would be men with the right connections extending every effort to learn Millicent's whereabouts. He started the sedan's motor and was about to put it in gear when he felt a touch of cold metal on the back of his neck.

"Keep your hands on the wheel," came a rasping voice.

Harvey kept his hands on the wheel, just in case. But he said: "Oh, it's you again. Now what?"

"You're under arrest!" said O'Reilly. "I'm going to take you down to headquarters and let the boys work over you—unless you'd rather cooperate and hand over those papers."

Harvey sighed deeply, and put the car into gear. Tentatively he eased out the clutch and moved the car a few feet.

"Hey! Where you going?" demanded the state cop.

"Down to headquarters," said Harvey, and grinned to himself as he felt the pressure of the gun removed.

"You're a hard man," complained O'Reilly, plaintively. "Why don't you give a guy a break? You were supposed to be scared and hand over the papers."

"I must have mislaid the script," said Harvey, smiling wryly.

"Look, Sherlock, why don't you go home for a few hours and get ready for a tough evening? Rest up a bit."

"Nothing doing," said O'Reilly. "As soon as I turn my back you'll give me the slip."

"Okay," said Harvey, wearily. "Let's go and get a bite to eat."

"On you?" suggested O'Reilly.

"On me," agreed Harvey.

PATELLI'S CLUB was a different place altogether, during the day. There wasn't any orchestra, blaring forth its alleged music. Nor was the air heavy with tobacco smoke and synthetic gayety. Harvey decided it would be a good place to eat, especially since he didn't want to risk missing Patelli's first call. There were plenty of vacant tables and he selected one over near the bar and its frozen-faced attendant.

Harvey Nelson was worried. He didn't know whether the night-club man would be able to learn anything, and he hated the inaction of waiting. But since he hadn't the slightest idea of how to locate Bonzetti's hideout, there was nothing else he could do. O'Reilly, watching his face, sensed that something was wrong.

"You look like you'd lost your best friend," he observed.

"Worse than that," said Harvey. "My girl."

O'Reilly clucked his tongue sympathetically. "What happened?"

"She said she couldn't cook sauerkraut," Harvey answered mournfully. "I said she'd have to learn, because I like sauer-kraut at least three times a week—with dumplings. She said she wouldn't, and—Well, one word led to another and…"

"Yeah," said O'Reilly. "You got to smack them around once in a while, or they begin to feel important. But you ought to waited till you married her."

"I guess I ought to have," agreed Harvey. "But you don't know how I love sauerkraut!"

The meal arrived at that moment, and the conversation fell

Pembroke shrieked. "He's dead!"
and began pumping bullets into
the approaching body of Bonzetti

flat on its face. Harvey was busy masticating a piece of steak, well done, while O'Reilly was trying to figure why he hadn't ordered sauerkraut.

Dessert had just been consumed when Patelli's call came. Harvey almost upset the table when the bartender beckoned to him.

"I've got something," came Patelli's voice over the phone. "I'll have things lined up by six o'clock. See me then."

Perhaps it was the meal which mellowed Mr. O'Reilly, but he didn't put up much of an argument when Harvey again suggested that he go home and rest up. He seemed to take Harvey at his word when Harvey swore that he intended to go back to his apartment and stay there until nearly six. O'Reilly waved a goodbye from the curb as Harvey drove off.

CHAPTER XXI

BACK TO TOMORROW

HARVEY PEELED OFF his jacket and hung it, with the vest, on a hanger in a closet. He was removing his necktie when he had his first inkling that everything was not as it should be. But then it was too late to do anything about it.

> *"How do you feel?"*
>
> *"Not much stronger."*
>
> *"Can you read minds yet? Is that guy O'Reilly on the up and up?"*
>
> *"I haven't been able to get into his mind yet, but I think he's all right."*
>
> *"Suppose he's really working with Inspector Schwartz instead of trying to get the jump on him?"*
>
> *"I don't think so. Considering the way Schwartz treated him."*
>
> *"But Schwartz said he was going to put a tail on Harvey. Where's the tail if it's not O'Reilly?"*
>
> *"You heard that when we first came back here in time. How do you know Schwartz said it again? We didn't stay to listen, you know. And I'm supposed to have changed history by interfering."*
>
> *"But everything else was just the same… Say! Look at that!"*

HARVEY HAD loosened the knot of his necktie and was in the act of slipping the loop over his head, when he saw a toe protruding from the bathroom doorway. At the same instant he saw a hand descending toward his head. He made a quick swipe at the hand, to knock it aside, but at that instant his thumb caught in the loop of the necktie.

The sudden jerk pulled his head forward, for the loop wasn't yet free. The blackjack in the descending hand was thus given a perfect target. Lightning exploded in Harvey's head and he knew no more.

"Stop them! Grab 'em!"

Omega tried, but it wasn't any use. He hadn't nearly the strength he had had when he'd first masqueraded as Harvey's shadow. He couldn't even trip the smaller of the men. Frantically he tried to impede their movements as one of them grabbed Harvey's coat and hastily went through the pockets. He tried mightily to exert enough pressure to knock one of them out, but the forces of nature no longer obeyed the mighty Omega. He was a shadow now, and shadows didn't indulge in such pastimes.

Mark hurled himself at the men also, but he passed through them without even slowing. Mark wasn't even a shadow.

"Harvey's unconscious," Omega said, as the marauders quietly closed the door behind them. "If he wasn't, I might have been able to do something."

"Why?"

"Simply because he knows I can exert force. He's seen me do it."

"That would make it so, eh? Why doesn't it work the other way around! You're a shadow because he believes it, aren't you? He's captured your thought pattern. So when he goes to sleep, that ought to release it."

"It would, if I had my strength. But this long stay in the past has weakened me. Now I need his belief in my powers in order to do anything."

"It doesn't make sense."

"Sure it does. Listen. Normally I derive all my power from my knowledge of how to manipulate the subcosmic forces which abound in all space and matter. You follow?"

"Sure I follow. I'm ahead. Those forces abound here, just the same. Even if you are six thousand years from your normal time. You used those same forces when you really existed during this period. So why can't you use them now? Have you forgotten how?"

"I haven't forgotten anything. The point is that these forces are wave motions, similar to light but smaller. They exist just as that table exists. And they weren't tapped or used at this time. Therefore they resist movement very strongly, for the simple reason that six

thousand years have passed and the fabric of time has become firmly set."

"You used them plenty when you first came back. You kicked Harvey all over the place."

"I know. But it gets harder all the time. I didn't realize that at first or I wouldn't have exerted myself. Each thing I did that hadn't really been done when that time had passed normally, stretched the fabric out of shape. Time is elastic, you know. So that each new thing I did caused a distortion which pushed against the normal shape of the fabric. Naturally, the further it was stretched the more it resisted. Do you grasp the analogy?"

"I think so. But what are you going to do?"

"Oh I'll strengthen a little when Harvey wakes up. His belief will increase the force I'm able to exert. But right now I'd better try to revive him. If I had strength enough to lift a glass of water. But I haven't. It takes half my energy to keep you here so that you can observe..."

Mark suddenly realized that everything was black, and the familiar sinking feeling had returned. There was an instant of panic, then he was angry. Omega had cast him off! He'd return automatically to his own time and wouldn't know what was happening to Harvey.

But he cooled off when he realized that Omega had only done it so that he would have sufficient strength to throw some water on Harvey and bring him to. When that was done, Omega would bring him back into the past again. He hoped.

Abruptly the sinking sensation ceased and Mark found himself at the bank of the creek. He was in his own body, completely alone. The water at his feet gurgled placidly among some small rocks at the edge of the bank. He watched it for a moment, thinking, then turned to look at the ravine which Omega had cut. He looked, but didn't see it. There was only a rolling prairie on all sides!

Puzzled, Mark lined up the little rise where Omega had started the cut. He could see the place, though it looked different from before. The sides of the cut had fallen in and grass had almost obliterated all evidence of its existence.

His eyes followed the place where the stream had diverted for a time; but it was almost impossible to distinguish it. Where silt hadn't covered it, the banks had fallen and grass covered it completely.

Mark suddenly sat down, staring at the rushing, bubbling water.

The whole excursion into time had accomplished nothing. He had gotten all excited about Harvey's plight and influenced Omega to take a hand, and it didn't mean a thing. Time went on, inexorably, and no amount of effort could change those things which had happened. Slight, impermanent alterations, perhaps, but in the main changing nothing.

Omega was wrong. There was some law governing the immutability of events, of which he was ignorant. It seemed incredible, but it was true. And that meant that so important an event as a murder could not be made not to happen. Nor could a man suspected of that murder be relieved of suspicion. Nor—

Mark jumped to his feet. Suppose Harvey were to endanger himself in his quest to find Millicent? Omega could not protect him. If he had been killed in the attempt, nothing Omega could do would prevent it. He might make changes, but they wouldn't affect the result. The methods, perhaps; but not the result.

Mark paced beside the creek. Even if he could do nothing to change events which had already happened, he still wished to observe them. He waited, impatiently, for Omega to reach ahead and draw him into the past.

CHAPTER XXII

ONE-SHOT PATELLI

A GLASS OF water floated through the air, stopped for a second as it hovered over Harvey's face, and emptied itself. Then it returned to the wash bowl in the bathroom, only a few feet away, and filled itself again. A wispy, almost diaphanous column of something resembling thin tobacco smoke appeared to be supporting the glass. It was more or less rigid and substantial, however, and refused to disperse, as real smoke would have done.

The glass returned to Harvey; but this time it didn't pour itself. It was about to, when the recumbent Mr. Nelson suddenly came to life, saw the glass and dodged aside.

This little maneuver caused stabs of pain to center in the region of the back of his head, and things began to go black again. He fought it off, concentrating on a mental picture of Millicent, who was in dire distress and needed his aid.

The urgency of the thought cleared his brain quickly. He sat up, and in doing so rested momentarily in a puddle of water. This finished the job, of bringing his mental processes to full recovery. He sprang to his feet, swayed dizzily, and rubbed his head.

"What happened?" he asked.

"We got conked," answered Omega.

"We?"

"Yeah," said Omega. "I was awake coming up the stairs, and I was about to say something. I think I was going to suggest that you put those papers in a safe place, when things blacked out."

Harvey suddenly quit rubbing his scalp. "The papers!" he

gasped, and made a dash for the closet where he had hung his coat. He went frantically from pocket to pocket, though he knew very well he was wasting his energy. The papers were gone, and there wasn't any sense looking in pockets where he hadn't put them. The envelope in which he had carried them had been too large to fit any but the inside pocket of his coat. And that pocket was empty.

He slumped in an upholstered chair, unmindful of the fact that he was soaking wet at the point of contact.

"It doesn't matter much," said Omega.

"What do you mean?"

"Simply that you have to find Milly anyway," said Omega, "Those papers wouldn't have helped."

Laboriously Harvey began removing his soggy clothes. A warm bath would make him feel better, he hoped. It was exactly five-fifty when he locked the door behind him. Then he turned toward his car, and stopped suddenly. O'Reilly was hunched in the back seat, sound asleep. Harvey shook him vigorously.

"Don't trust me, eh?" he commented.

The State cop rubbed his eyes, reluctantly coming back to the world of the living. "Trust you!" he said. "After the trick you tried to pull?"

"What trick?"

"Oh, you kept your promise, all right. You didn't leave your place till now, just like you said. But it was a trick just the same. Visitors—that you didn't want me to know about."

Harvey stopped suddenly, his foot poised over the starter button. "What visitors?" he snapped.

"As if you didn't know," derided O'Reilly. "I was suspicious of the way you tried to get rid of me. So I followed in a cab. I watched your door for a while, and then the two guys came out."

"Who?" yelled Harvey, turning in his seat. "Who were they?"

O'Reilly's eyes widened. He suddenly realized that Harvey was serious, that he really didn't know who his visitors had been.

"Lucky Bonzetti, and one of his gang," he said, mystified. "What's the matter now?"

Harvey had growled, deep in his throat. Bonzetti had been in his own flat, practically in his hands, and held let him get away. If he'd kept his wits about him, Millicent might be free by now. But he'd been caught flat-footed.

THE PATTERN of events seemed to fall into place. As soon as Harvey had left Pembroke's offices, Bonzetti had been put to work to recover the papers. There wasn't any use reviling himself now; the thing was done, and Millicent wouldn't have been safe anyway, papers or no papers. But it was all the more urgent that he find her, now that Pembroke had them. They at least had afforded a guarantee of her safety until after the primaries.

"What's it all about, Mr. Nelson?" asked O'Reilly. "This business is driving me loco."

"Bonzetti knocked me out," Harvey revealed. "He took those papers."

"You mean the ones you took off Dolly Patterson?" asked O'Reilly slyly.

Harvey's grin was something of a grimace. "Get up here in the front seat," he said. "Now I'm going to tell you some things. Mainly so that you'll know what's going on, in case I need your help."

Harvey talked rapidly. By the time he pulled up in front of Patelli's club, he had imparted practically all the information necessary to give O'Reilly a working knowledge of what had been going on. He judicially left out all mention of the machinations of Omega, who was a hard individual to explain.

The doorman informed them that Patelli hadn't arrived yet, though he was expected any minute. Harvey thanked him and led O'Reilly toward the bar.

"Then you figure Bonzetti killed Dolly Patterson?" O'Reilly asked.

"You're the detective," said Harvey. "All I want to do is to find

Miss Forbes. And, once she's safe, get Fowler elected. Though that's unimportant right now."

"Sure. I'm with you on that," said O'Reilly. "But I also want to know how it ties up with the death of Dolly Patterson. You're only guessing when you figure Pembroke put Bonzetti on the job of getting those papers from you. I figure he put him on the job while she still had them. He botched the job. Killed her, and then couldn't find the hiding place."

"Could be," admitted Harvey. "Let's have a drink."

> *"You're stronger, eh? It didn't take you long to bring me back."*
>
> *"A little. I revived Nelson with water. Then I got stronger as soon as he woke up and saw me doing it. I'm not what I ought to be, though."*
>
> *"You never were. Can you get away from him yet?"*
>
> *"No. He's too firmly convinced we're inseparable. Something has to happen to change his mind. Unless I get a lot stronger—I'll have to give it some thought."*

THE BARTENDER produced a bottle with a kilted Highlander on the label, and shoved it across the bar. Harvey saw O'Reilly lick his lips as he filled his glass. He also saw him frown slightly at the small glasses of seltzer which followed. O'Reilly, slugged down the drink and watched Harvey pour his into the seltzer and stir it gently.

"Sissy," he said, pouring himself another.

"Brain-work," countered Harvey. "I can drink twice as many by diluting them."

"That's not brain-work," O'Reilly disagreed. "It's extravagance. I can get pie-eyed at half the cost, by drinking them straight."

A buzzer sounded behind the bar. The bartender put a small head-phone to his ear.

"Mr. Patelli's in the office," he said.

Harvey looked at O'Reilly thoughtfully. "You stay here," he said.

"I'll go with you."

"No. Stay here. Patelli mightn't like the idea of—All right, come along."

Nelson led the way to Patelli's office. The night-club proprietor looked askance at the man in the rumpled blue suit. Nor did he seem quite satisfied when Harvey introduced him as Mr. O'Reilly.

"Is that all?" he inquired. "Just 'mister'? I think I've seen that Irish pan before."

"Is that guy insulting me?" O'Reilly asked.

"You wouldn't know," said Patelli, looking at Harvey. "He's a cop, huh?"

Harvey looked uncomfortable. He realized he should have told Patelli the truth in the first place.

"Yes," he admitted. "He's been following me ever since last night. I couldn't get rid of him, so I enlisted his aid. What did you find out?"

Patelli regarded O'Reilly with a certain amount of distaste. "Wait a minute," he said. "I don't like this cop business. I never got anything but trouble from cops. They rob you and then they raid you anyway. They're not to be trusted. They're dishonest."

O'Reilly, already of somewhat ruddy complexion, threatened to burst into flame.

"It doesn't matter," Harvey said quickly. "Nothing you're going to say could be used to embarrass you. What did you learn?"

"Yeah, that's right," Patelli admitted. "Here's some addresses. One of them ought to be the one you want."

He shoved a typewritten paper across the desk. Harvey looked at the list of addresses. "Why so many?" he asked.

"For his boys, I guess," Patelli hazarded. "He probably pays their rent. The trick is to pick out the right one. I can't help you there. This Bonzetti is a cagey guy. All we dug up, except from these addresses, was some dope on a few jobs he pulled in the past."

"What dope was that?" asked O'Reilly.

"THERE YOU are, Mr. Nelson," said Patelli, regarding O'Reilly with a cold eye. "I told you a cop's not to be trusted. He wants to go off on a side track, just to collect a record for himself."

But Harvey wasn't listening. He was going down the list of addresses.

"Bonzetti would have the most pretentious place for himself," he deduced. "Here's one. An apartment at the Thyssen Arms."

"Be a tough place to conceal a kidnapped girl," said Patelli. "How about that house on Thirteenth Street? A house would be the place to keep a prisoner."

Harvey lifted his eyes from the list and stared at the blank wall bewilderedly. This was the worst quandary he'd ever been in. The address where Milly was imprisoned was right before him, and he was mortally afraid to pick it out. If he missed, there was every chance that Bonzetti would be warned, with possible disastrous results to Milly. At the very least Bonzetti would leave, and then there might be no lead at all to follow. His eyes returned to the list, blurred slightly, then focused again.

"How about that place in the country?" suggested Patelli. "At the bottom of the list."

Harvey shook his head. He was hearing another voice, as Patelli spoke, and this one pointed a way out of his dilemma.

"Try the house in town," Omega said. "It's probably his home. Someone's bound to be there, even if it isn't the right place. Maybe I can do a little mind-reading for you."

"The house it is," said Harvey, looking at Patelli. "I want to thank you, Joe. This means—"

"Forget it," said Patelli. "You're not counting me out yet. I'll go along." He patted a bulge in his coat, near the armpit. "I'm still pretty handy with this thing."

O'Reilly snorted. "An Eyetalian couldn't hit a telephone booth if he was inside it," he contended.

Patelli didn't deny this assertion. He didn't even look angry. But there was a sudden explosion in the vicinity of his hand, and the cigarette in O'Reilly's fingers shortened itself by half. The trooper allowed his jaw to relax slightly, then calmly lit the remains of the cigarette.

"Your old lady must have been scared by an Irishman," he remarked.

Patelli extended him a fresh pack, smiling. "There must have been a Scotch boarder in your house," he said. "Have a whole one."

CHAPTER XXIII

THE DEAD WALK: STARRING OMEGA

BONZETTI'S HOUSE WAS in one of the better sections of the city, a half-hour's drive from Patelli's club. All three men realized that they were heading into something they wouldn't be able to back out of. Bonzetti's place might be well guarded, and their approach noted and prepared for. But all three were gambling on the fact that Bonzetti was known to have a small compact gang, and therefore wouldn't likely have more than one or two men posted.

The house, situated in the center of well-kept lawns, was darkened when they arrived. There wasn't a light to be seen at any window. This, Patelli pointed out, didn't mean that no one was home. Drapes might be over the windows of any room with a light in it.

"We'll take it head on," Harvey said. "I'll bang on the door and when it opens, you cover whoever answers it."

"Might as well," agreed Patelli. "There won't be any unlocked windows."

It was an excellent plan, except that didn't work. The whole thing rested on quick action when the door opened. But the door didn't open! Harvey found a push-button. He pushed it. And then he banged once more with his fist.

"Maybe there's nobody home," said O'Reilly.

Patelli raised his eyebrows. "Somebody told you, Irish."

Back in the car, as Harvey took out the list of addresses, Omega seized the opportunity to make another mental suggestion. "Try that place at the bottom of the list. Strikes me as being the next most likely."

Harvey relayed the decision as his own, and started the car. He realized now that even a wrong guess was better than inaction. He couldn't forget that Bonzetti possessed the only guarantee of Millicent's continued safety.

HARVEY'S SEDAN, in the next half-hour, proved that the manufacturers hadn't been exaggerating a bit. It roared along at a rate which ate up the miles with gusto and sound effects. Harvey was familiar with the surrounding countryside, and could almost visualize the exact location of the house.

His tires screamed a protest as he turned abruptly into a rough side road. From that point on the car went at a crawl, with the lights turned out. He drove cautiously, a thin crescent of a moon preventing a collision with the trees which lined the path. Long before he reached the spot where, the car might be visible from the house, he stopped clear of the road and opened the door.

"End of the line," he said tersely. "We'd better walk from here. It must be pretty close. Keep your eyes open."

Harvey led the way through the trees, abandoning the road. Less than a hundred yards from where they'd left the car, they saw Bonzetti's house—a bungalow.

A lighted floor-lamp was visible in the living room but there was no sign of activity. The rest of the place was dark.

"Give me your gun, O'Reilly," said Harvey.

"Yeah, give him your gun, Irish," said Patelli. "You wouldn't know what to do with it anyway."

"Quiet!" whispered Harvey. "And stay put, I'm going to look in that window!"

Harvey stalked the window, not making a sound. When he reached it, he cautiously moved until he could look through. And in the range of his vision he saw enough to make him swear softly in surprise. Sprawled on the floor, his back to the window, was a man—or what had been one. A pool of dark blood surrounded the head.

Across the room, almost out of sight, was another body. This one was visible only from the hips down, the rest concealed behind a large chair. Harvey frantically twisted to the opposite side of the window, trying to see more of the room. But no other body was visible.

"Come on!" he yelled, and dashed for the front door.

The door was unlocked and he pounded in, no longer caring whether he made noise or not. A quick glance showed that no one else was in the living room. He leaped over one of the bodies and headed for the next room. He found a light switch, but that room was empty also. Room after room brought the same result. Millicent wasn't in the bungalow.

He returned to the living room, panting and almost sobbing. Patelli and O'Reilly had come in the front door and were staring at the two bodies.

"Deader than my club in the daytime," pronounced Patelli. "That one's Bonzetti. I don't know this guy. One of his hoods. Wonder who chilled them."

"That ain't the point," said O'Reilly. "Where's Nelson's girl? Not in the house, eh?"

Harvey shook his head.

"Maybe *she* got the jump on them somehow," Patelli suggested.

"Not likely," said Harvey. "She wouldn't have shot them. But she might have escaped! Go get the car. I want to do some thinking."

Harvey suddenly slumped in an overstuffed chair, head buried in his hands. The two men looked at him for a second, then went out to get the car. As soon as they left he jumped up and crossed the room. Not far from the body of Bonzetti he leaned over and picked up a large manila envelope.

"Oh-oh," grunted Omega. "It looks as if Bonzetti tried to hold up the leader of your great party. He must have got those lists on his own hook, or a price would have been agreed upon. Though how he knew about them is more than I can say."

"O'Reilly might have guessed right when he said that Pembroke might have hired him to recover them from Dolly Patterson," Harvey said. "Or he might have told him about them to explain why he had to keep his hands off Milly. But right now we've got to find… Say! Pembroke must have taken her with him. He still needs her to guarantee the votes of the Fifty-second. Omega, do me a favor. Inhabit Bonzetti's body!"

"What! Make a ghoul out of myself?"

"You've *got* to! It's the only way we can jar Pembroke into doing something rash. The way things stand we can't prove a thing. And he's got Milly!"

"Oh all right," agreed Omega, reluctantly.

> *"That'll take a lot of power. Dead men don't walk, as a general rule. Can you do it?"*
>
> *"This is what I've been waiting for! Don't you see? Harvey is perfectly sure that I can do it. There's no doubt in his mind. I've done practically the same thing before. I'm getting stronger every minute.*
>
> *"The fact that it's a dead body don't mean a thing. Harvey knows it's dead, all right; but when the others see it move they'll think Bonzetti was only wounded. And their minds won't work against me. Watch!"*

CHAPTER XXIV

KEEP TUNED TO THIS STATION

THE HACKLES ROSE on Harvey's neck, even though it was his own idea, when the body of Bonzetti rolled over on its face and drew the knees up to rise. He controlled his feelings, though, with the thought that it was only Omega manipulating a bunch of meat instead of the usual assortment of clothes.

"He's kind of stiff," said Omega. "I'll have to limber him up."

At that moment Harvey heard the sound of his car driving up to the house. "Put on an act," he said. "We'll have to get you washed up. Pretend you were just wounded. I'll get a hat to cover that hole in your cranium."

Patelli gasped as he saw Harvey help the stiffly walking Bonzetti toward the bathroom. Automatically he removed his gun from its holster, pointing it at the gangster.

"He was only creased," Harvey called, "We'll take him with us."

Patelli kept the gun centered from the doorway as Harvey carefully cleaned most of the blood from Bonzetti's head. Cold shivers ran up his back as he performed the task; but he remembered to keep the punctured side of the head away from the door.

When he finished, after spoiling several towels, the result wasn't bad at all. Bonzetti must have fallen too quickly for any of the blood to splash his clothes. There were only a few spots on his collar.

"Stand there," he said, "I'll get your hat."

Harvey sidled past Patelli, ostensibly so that he wouldn't

block his gun, while Omega kept the body erect, with the wound away from the door. Bonzetti's face was twitching slightly as its occupant tried to get the face muscles working, but Patelli only saw a man groggy with shock and grimacing with pain. He didn't suspect a thing, naturally; and when Harvey returned with the hat, the evidence was effectively covered.

O'Reilly turned pale as Bonzetti stumbled stiffly out of the bungalow. "Holy Sunday!" he exclaimed. "I thought he was dead!"

"He had a pretty close call," Harvey said. "We're taking him back. You drive."

"Who shot you, Bonzetti?" O'Reilly demanded.

Omega tried to manipulate Bonzetti's vocal chords to say the name "Pembroke," but they refused to cooperate. He merely achieved a hoarse croak which didn't sound like anything, except perhaps a hoarse croak.

"He said he thinks it was Pembroke, but he's not sure," interpreted Harvey.

"We'll call on that gentleman, and try to get something out of him."

UNDER O'REILLY'S skillful hands the sedan performed almost as well as his own motorcycle. If anything it made better time than it had on the outward journey. Harvey sat beside Omega, in the rear seat, and tried to control the shivers which kept coursing their way up and down his spinal column every time a curve threw Bonzetti's remains off balance. He placed his borrowed gun on the seat beside him. It was a forty-five and too heavy to carry in a pocket when it wasn't necessary to do so.

This fact led to a discovery which made Omega feel a little optimistic. For when they alighted in front of Pembroke's home, Harvey helped Omega and his troublesome body out of the car, then turned back to retrieve the gun. Omega didn't notice this and kept on walking.

Harvey had decided in the car that Omega would place himself at the side of the door, out of sight, and then suddenly confront Pembroke in an effort to shatter that man's usually unbreakable poise. But Omega had barely crossed the sidewalk and started up the tree-lined path, when he suddenly collapsed.

Patelli, who had been watching alertly, gun pointed through a pocket, caught him as he fell. Harvey turned; but before he had reached the body, Omega had it on its feet again.

"A fine thing," he said, in Harvey's brain. "Why don't you stay—Say, how far away was I when I started to fall?"

"Almost thirty feet," answered Harvey.

Harvey's knock and repeated rings on the door bell brought no sign of life. The Pembroke home was apparently deserted, even by the servants. Harvey helped Omega fold himself back in the car.

"The Bugle Building," he directed.

Once more O'Reilly slammed the car into motion. Patelli kept his gun pointed at Bonzetti's mid-section, though the gangster's body had made no show of wanting to be elsewhere. He was, in fact, a very sick-looking corpse, with an extremely unhealthy color.

The elevator boy in the Bugle Building looked very startled when Harvey laid a heavy hand on his shoulder. But he promised to go up as slowly as possible when Harvey explained that Mr. Bonzetti was a very sick man and couldn't stand any jolting starts or stops. He could readily see that the man was sick. Cheating an undertaker, was the way he privately expressed it.

"What are you figuring on doing?" asked O'Reilly. "If Bonzetti ain't sure, we better not pull anything rough. Pembroke is a pretty hot guy."

"You said you would string along with me," Harvey reminded. "So stay out of the office when I go in. I want Pembroke to see Bonzetti without any warning."

PEMBROKE LOOKED up and scowled as Nelson walked in, half suspecting that he meant no good by his visit. Harvey stopped in front of the desk.

"Where is she?" he asked, shortly.

"What's come over you?" demanded Pembroke in a soft voice. "Our agreement still stands. After election you'll get her back.

"I want her now," said Harvey. "You have her. You took her with you when you got the lists from Bonzetti."

Pembroke looked slightly startled at the emphasis Harvey put on the last word. His hand reached in the upper drawer of the desk and brought out a gun. He smiled—almost cheerfully.

"Go ahead," he said. "Speak your piece. You've come in here with blood in your eye often enough for me to be able to prove you've been threatening—"

Pembroke's eyes shifted momentarily, then fixed themselves in the direction of the door. His gloating expression turned to one of stark incredulity. Then, in the twinkling of an eye, he lost all his rigid self-control. His mouth worked, trying to form syllables. Then he shrieked: "He's dead!" and swung the gun toward the approaching body of Bonzetti, pumping shot after shot into it. The menacing figure wilted and slumped to the floor.

Harvey was ready to dive across the table before Pembroke could recover from his fright, but it wasn't necessary. A single shot exploded from the region of the door. Pembroke's gun clattered to the floor; he dazedly grasped at the torn remnant of the hand which had held it, then moaned and sank down in his chair.

O'Reilly walked in, closely followed by Patelli.

"That wasn't a bad shot, Irish," the latter commented. "Though it seems to me his head would have made a better target."

"I meant to hit his hand," claimed O'Reilly. "Now we can fry him in the chair, too. It's more sporting."

Harvey was bent over Bonzetti's body, his ear pressed close to the stiffened lips. Bewilderment and something akin to grief was mirrored in his eyes.

During the instant following the reverberation of O'Reilly's shot, Harvey had heard his name called, weakly and appealingly. Omega! But it hadn't come from within his brain or beside his ear. It had come from the fallen body of Bonzetti! Unbelievingly he had kneeled, and heard: "Give Milly my best…"

"How's that for an exit?" exclaimed Omega triumphantly, as he and Mark whirled through the blackness to their own time.

Mark lurched dizzily as he again found himself in his own body, back at the edge of the creek.

"In the middle of the second act!" he yelled. "What happened? Who killed Dolly Patterson? Bonzetti?"

Omega, once more garbed in flowing Roman toga, a beret and spiked shoes, looked surprised. "Don't you know?" he asked innocently.

Mark tried to answer, but the words got jammed in his throat.

"Pembroke, of course," Omega continued. "Dolly Patterson knew when she had a good thing. She wanted Pembroke to pay and pay. Not for the lists, mind you, but just so she wouldn't publish them. And Pembroke couldn't stand being on the wrong end of a black-mail scheme.

"Bonzetti named too high a price to recover them, so Pembroke went after them himself. Lost his head when Dolly wouldn't listen to reason, and killed her. But that's how Bonzetti knew about the lists. He must have tricked Milly into admitting that Harvey had found them. And Bonzetti got the same medicine as Dolly when he tried to squeeze Pembroke."

"How do you know all that?"

"From Pembroke's mind, just before he shot me."

Mark groaned. "The police can't read minds. Schwartz will still—"

"Don't worry about Harvey," Omega interrupted. "O'Reilly knows Dolly Patterson was murdered for those lists. And the lists themselves incriminate Pembroke, not Harvey. Schwartz will forget his suspicions when he sees them."

Mark nodded. "Milly and he will probably get married right away."

"Yeah," Omega drawled. "They will. Six thousand years ago."

Mark nodded again. Then suddenly: "Let's go back and see how they get along—"

He stopped. Omega was dwindling before his eyes. A wispy, almost diaphanous column of something resembling thin tobacco smoke rose from the ground.

Mark braced himself, but it was too late. He felt himself hurled into the air; turned several somersaults and finally landed flat on his back in the grass. There was a gleeful chuckle, followed by a shivering, quivering sound which sounded like an enormous dishpan being hit.

"THE SHADOW STRIKES!" came a sepulchral voice, as the vibration of the dishpan died to a whisper.

www.ingramcontent.com/pod-product-compliance
Lightning Source LLC
Chambersburg PA
CBHW030532020726
47494CB00004B/1329